T0099474

# FAITHFUL REBECCA

# FAITHFUL REBECCA

*A NOVEL BY* *JANICE EIDUS*

*FICTION COLLECTIVE* *NEW YORK · BOULDER*

*Library of Congress Cataloguing in Publication Data*

*Eidus, Janice*
  *Faithful Rebecca*

*I. Title*
*PS3555.I38F3    1987    813.'54    86-29564*
*ISBN: 0-932-51106-6*
*ISBN: 0-932-51107-4 (pbk.)*

*Published by Fiction Collective with assistance from the*
*National Endowment for the Arts; the support of the Publications*
*Center, University of Colorado, Boulder; and with the*
*cooperation of Brooklyn College, Illinois State University*
*and Teachers & Writers Collaborative.*

*Grateful acknowledgement is also made to the Graduate School,*
*the School of Arts and Sciences, and the President's Fund of*
*the University of Colorado, Boulder.*

*The author expresses deep gratitude to Raymond Federman for*
*his generosity.*

*The author also thanks the MacDowell Colony, The Corporation*
*of Yaddo, The Millay Colony for the Arts, and the Virginia*
*Center for the Creative Arts for their assistance.*

*Manufactured in the United States of America*

*Typeset by Fisher Composition, Inc.*

*Designed by Abe Lerner*

*This book is for John Kastan*

*"How do you know but ev'ry
Bird that cuts the airy way,
Is an immense world of delight,
clos'd by your senses five?"*
                    *—William Blake*

# I

Rebecca awoke, unsure whether she'd been asleep for hours, days, or weeks. She was confident that she would awaken to the sight of Sagana, that Sagana would be standing above her, about to feed her a spoonful of soothing homemade soup, because Sagana had been nursing her back to health from this debilitating fever. She could imagine the soup that Sagana would carefully spoon into her lips—a creamy pink soup of yogurt and cucumbers.

But Sagana's voice had changed, Rebecca thought. Now it was like a man's voice, like a young boy's, actually. This new voice was kind of pleasant, and so she smiled, one of her first conscious acts since arriving on the mountain . . . yet something disturbed her, this new boyish voice wasn't as friendly as it could have been, not loving at all. Rebecca slowly opened her eyes.

"Well, what's been going on with you?" asked the teenaged boy seated in front of her. He looked up from the three long leather straps he was braiding together. He sounded bored.

A brat, Rebecca thought. Not Sagana, but some bratty kid.

His long sandy-colored hair had split ends from the crown to the uneven edges. He wore overalls which were baggy and soiled and patched with multi-colored bits of fabric and small oval mirrors. He appeared naked underneath. She was attracted, despite her will and the fever, to his flesh. To his tanned skin. But he struck her—even in her haze—as the kind of spoiled brat who occasionally sauntered into the restaurant where she used to waitress, thinking that the combination of his wisecracks and baby blue eyes would impress her.

She hadn't liked waitressing, and Sagana had liked the work even less. But they needed work after college, and neither had any inclination toward pursuing a genuine career. "Certainly not graduate school," Rebecca had scoffed. "Imagine me—stuck in a library all day . . ."

"I hate to think of pretty you stuck anywhere," Sagana had agreed.

Now Rebecca stared more closely at the young boy in front of her. His skin was lovely and smooth, and she'd always liked touching soft skin, skin like her own.

Was Sagana's skin smooth, soft? She couldn't remember through the fever, but doubted it. In high school Sagana had developed acne, although not the sort that left crevices and purple blots. Rebecca had always been grateful for that.

The boy resumed working at his leather straps.

"Where's Sagana?" Rebecca managed, finding it a huge effort to speak at all. Much more natural would have been drifting back into the delirium of the fever.

He shrugged, letting go of the leather straps and creating an imaginary drum riff in the air with his fingers. "Sagana? Who dat?"

"Moron," responded Rebecca, immediately surprised by her own childishness. Often, back in grade school, she'd made similar retorts to the boys in the schoolyard when they'd teased her about her friendship with Sagana, even though she knew that they were just jealous. And on that afternoon when one had called out, "Hey, Rebecca, the Poison Insecta, where's your little friend?" as she hurried by on the way to the super-market for her mother, she'd screamed, "Moron! Drop dead! Creep!"

"Hey, you're still delirious," the boy now answered, "I'm no moron, I've got an I.Q. way way up there . . ." His eyebrows lifted and he stared heavenward.

Cretin, thought Rebecca, focusing on the way his fingers braided the three tan strips of leather.

"No, seriously, folks," he went on, putting aside the three strips, "what for you on this mountain, and what for you want this here Sagana?"

"She's my best friend!"

Leaning back, hands and fingers still, expression impassive, he pronounced, "Hmm . . . I see . . ."

"She's my best friend. And she has my . . . child . . . here with her!"

"Them's the breaks, lady." He threw an imaginary ball into an imaginary basket. "Hey, two points for me!"

"Who are you?"

"God, not again!" He faked a long yawn. "Who am I? Same old song . . . you think because I'm only six-teen I have an identity problem. But I don't. I know exactly who I am. I am not Howard Geller, the kid who stuttered around his father's business cronies when they tried talking baseball to him. I don't live on East End Avenue. And I don't attend the Dalton School. Why do you think you know anything about me? You don't know me at all."

"Look, please just tell Sagana that I'm here. Please tell her!" Something's very wrong, she felt, if this boy can remain so callous, despite my beauty and frailty . . . "She'd want to be with me if she knew I was sick, and she'd want me to be with my own . . . baby!"

9

He stood up, swooping up the straps with a theatrical flourish. "And I'm telling you for the last time that not only do I not know this Howard Geller, I don't know this Sagana either."

As he exited through the opening in the hut that served as a door, he turned around once before disappearing. "And I sure don't know any Evan, this guy you keep calling for." He grinned, twirled around, leapt up and pretended to shoot another basket. "Hey, two more points for me!"

The boy who was not Howard Geller hadn't returned to the hut in what seemed to Rebecca like days. Although she felt hungry, she wasn't able to do more than sit up for a few minutes at a time. When she tried to stand, feeling a need to hunt down some food—even more important now than finding Sagana, Evan, or Lily— she would swoon. She tried to familiarize herself with her surroundings: with the bumps and valleys of the hut's dirt floor, with the circular domed top, with the stone walls, with the patterns formed in the dirt, the patterns formed in the stone. She missed the familiar objects of her apartment back home in New York City. She'd always felt safest, most secure, when surrounded by stereos, television sets, radios, bookcases loaded to capacity, vases crammed with dried flowers, electric blenders, and of course her collection of dolls. She'd had the dolls since she was a child.

Noise too had always been a comfort: honking cars, shouting street vendors, sirens . . . but now there were few sounds other than her own. She could hear nothing outside the hut other than the occasional scurrying of what sounded like a small animal, and once or twice the distant calling of birds. Perhaps it had been a mistake to leave everything behind, to fly off into the night, attempting to track down Sagana and Evan and Lily. Sagana wanted nothing more to do with her, ever again. Why else would she have run off and taken Lily to this crazy place? But if she'd truly never intended to be followed, why had she left that piece of paper? On the floor, next to their refrigerator, Rebecca had discovered the crumbled piece of notepaper with Sagana's whereabouts written on it.

She looked around the hut. Her pocketbook was there, and her comb, and toothbrush. But her suitcase was gone, and with it her mirror. She panicked, wondering if the filth on her skin would obliterate her beauty forever. Perhaps that was why the boy who was not Howard Geller was so hostile.

The fever lingered. She still couldn't stand up. Then, while she was sleeping deeply, Sagana came and stood above her. Rebecca awoke, unclear—had she been dreaming? But now there were three white envelopes neatly arranged beside her. They were unopened. Slowly she understood. They were her own letters to Sagana, the letters she had imagined herself dramatically composing before a camera, the letters alternately begging and commanding Sagana to reveal why she'd run off with Lily to a mountain commune. She'd begun writing the letters on the very day she discovered the paper by the refrigerator with Sagana's destination written on it. And now the letters had turned up beside her, neatly stacked and unopened. Sagana had never read a single line. But at least she had real proof now that Sagana was on the mountain! Something else had also been left behind, she realized. Fruits and vegetables and nuts of all sorts in a large basket: white mushrooms, huge ripe pears, crimson apples, cashews that nearly sparkled. There was so much food. She began to eat, slowly and deliberately. She was furious that Sagana had never read the letters.

Rebecca opened the first envelope and began to re-read the letter.

*Dear Sagana,*

*Too many pressing engagements up there on the mountain? No time to write, what with washing baby clothes in the stream and picking mushrooms?*

*The other day, I ran into your sister Miranda. We were both on our way into Penn Station. She was loaded down with Macy's shopping bags. I helped her carry them. She mentioned that you don't write to her either, and so I reprimand you doubly, and insist that you not forget sisterly love! After all, she and I are both, in quite different ways, sisters whom you have abandoned.*

*Miranda says that things are going nicely for her, her house is being redecorated, and her little son can say Mama. But you do remember that afternoon when you were babysitting for her, and you took her into your parents' bedroom with us? She was so much smaller than you. She was trembling. "Take your blouse off," you told her. Miranda screamed. "Nobody will hear you," you laughed. "Undress."*

*Miranda didn't move, and I rushed to her and ripped her blouse, with its Gulliver's Travels design, from her skinny chest. Then, as she wept, I drew circles around her tiny nipples with your mother's Vibrant Red lipstick.*

*"Now take off your shorts!" you commanded, never looking at me.*

*Miranda obeyed, allowing them to slip slowly down her stick legs, revealing panties that said, "I Love Grandma."*

*"You can leave those on," you decided. "I like them."*
*After her bellybutton was adorned with Vibrant Red, I*
*pulled down those panties a few inches and I drew circles*
*and stars and half-moons.*
    *Dazed, Miranda stared at the ceiling while I drew.*
*"Dance!" you demanded of her when I was done.*
    *I sang:*
            *Enter Miranda*
            *Come on and dance*
            *You've already dropped your pants*
            *So be like your sister*
            *And like me!*
*You ran into the kitchen and returned, pounding on a*
*frying pan and chanting words to a song of your own:*
            *Enter Miranda*
            *Sweet little dolly*
            *Be jolly, little lolly,*
            *Come be my sister*
            *And dance!*
    *Do you remember Miranda taking her first tentative*
*steps, a few little bunny hops in your direction? But then*
*we all heard that key in the door.*
    *"I'm telling Arnie!" yelled Miranda.*
    *"If you tell," you whispered, "I'll kill you, Miranda,"*
*and you spit out her name the way the demented circus*
*owner on "The Twilight Zone" had spit out the names of*
*his victims the night before.*
    *Miranda ran from the room, leaving us alone together*
*except for one of the cats—the Siamese—who had wan-*
*dered in. We stood together in your parents' bedroom*
*with Miranda's abandoned blouse, Lilliputian side up,*
*on the floor between us, and her cream-colored short-*
*shorts somehow entwined around my ankles.*
    *Well, Sagana, I meant to ask Miranda if she ever feels*

*guilty. Because she told, and she should feel guilty, she truly should. She told your older brother Arnie, home from school with his sneer and Elvis hairdo. Arnie saw Miranda, his fragile, favorite sister, running toward him. Miranda was sobbing terrible things about Sagana (the gawky sister he didn't like at all) and her conceited friend, Rebecca, the one who always thought she was better than everyone.*

*Remember how the bedroom door flew open and he stood, framed, eyes taking in the two of us at once.*

*"What's with you?" he asked, letting go of me with his eyes, staring only at you.*

*"Nothing. What's with you?"*

*"I should knock the shit out of you!"*

*Sagana, I remember exactly how you looked then, your brown eyes suddenly seeming smaller than ever behind your thick glasses, one of your long braids falling forward.*

*"It was me, Arnie!" I cried. "I did it!"*

*"Then I should knock the shit out of both of you!" But an idea came to Arnie so quickly then that we both knew it wasn't the first time. "I could tell Daddy and he'd think you were sick! That you girls were sick and he wouldn't let you two see each other again. He wouldn't let her sleep over ever again!"*

*"We're not sick," you countered. "You were born sicker than we are!"*

*"Yeah, yeah, maybe . . ." He grinned. I remember that grin. "But I won't do it, and I won't even lay a finger on you," he turned from you and suddenly focused on me, "if she comes into the staircase with me now."*

*"You're nuts." How final your voice was.*

*"Man, you know what Daddy would do to you, if I*

14

*told him. You'd be dead, he'd beat you bloody, black and blue, and your little girlfriend here, your best little girlfriend, wouldn't be allowed a mile from you!"*

*I closed my eyes. "Okay. I'll go."*

*Sagana, your eyes had become so strange by the time—a second later—I'd opened mine and looked at you. Squinting and shocked, angry, pained, loving, disbelieving, and then simply no longer there: behind your fogged eyeglasses they had vanished.*

*Arnie strode with teenaged confidence from the room. And you do remember, certainly, that I followed quickly and closed the door behind me.*

*Faithfully,*
*Rebecca*

As the letter slipped through her fingers, she thought how faithful she had been, but how she had been betrayed. How could that letter not have moved Sagana, if only she'd been willing to read it? Why hadn't Sagana wanted to hear from her? After all, she was lucky that Rebecca was only writing letters. She probably could have had Sagana arrested for kidnapping her daughter. But of course Sagana had known that Rebecca would never do that.

She'd hated running into Miranda that day, Miranda with her pug nose and sensible button earrings. Rebecca wondered if Arnie had ever confided in Miranda—later on, when they were older—what had gone on in the staircase.

She'd never before touched a boy. Yet many afternoons while she and Sagana played with the dolls, she would ache, fantasizing about something as yet unknown. . . about cowboy heroes, about sleek black sharks with sharp white teeth.

Arnie strode into the staircase, and she followed timidly behind. He stopped on one of the top steps and turned around. Rebecca stood, heart thumping, hands folded over her stomach. She stared at a glob of saliva on one of the lower steps.

"Your stomach hurt?" Arnie asked.

Rebecca dropped her hands, aware as she did so that now he was staring at her breasts. "Boobs," as Sagana said, to which Rebecca objected, wanting everything sexual—even then—to be cloaked in the loveliest language. "They're breasts, Saggie," she'd advise. "Breasts are beautiful, not boobs. Listen, the body is beautiful!" she cried, at age twelve. "That's going to be our motto, Saggie. Beauty above all!"

And now Arnie was staring at her body. "I'm only twelve," she murmured.

"So what?" said Arnie. "C'mere."

Rebecca moved slowly, thinking, "This is it, Becky. The beginning."

"How far have you gone?" Arnie asked.

"Nowhere," she answered.

"Nowhere? Now you're going somewhere. Open your mouth."

She did, and felt his tongue descend inside. And after that, she felt his fingers taking a determined path from her shoulders down the side of her arm, then beneath her blouse. And it was all so lovely. Not the best, not the most real, not nearly as far as she would go someday, but lovely nevertheless. She felt very much like one of her own female dolls—Black-Haired-Bazooka-Baby, Aunt Moonlight, Lola Lips—helpless, being toyed with, at the whim of some greater, powerful figure. She and Saggie were the ones who forced the dolls to do things, but now it was Arnie treating her like a mindless doll and this was what she craved. She loved it. Loved the pretense of being simple, of not caring what he did to her, of allowing him to take advantage of her and feel like a real man. But all the time she adored it, wanting him to do more, to be braver, to take full advantage. Which he didn't. Because he was, after all, only sixteen and a virgin himself, and she was his younger sister's best friend. When he had done as much as he seemed to know how, he sent her away.

"Button your blouse and go home," he ordered. "And don't go near Miranda, or I'll do this a second time!"

Rebecca flew down the stairs, racing the ten blocks to her own home, impatiently riding the elevator upstairs in time for dinner. At dinner, she and her mother and father were silent, as usual. She was thrilled with herself. Too excited to eat, she claimed a cold. "I've got to go to bed. If Sagana calls, just tell her I'm too sick to come to the phone."

But Sagana didn't call, which Rebecca found very strange, so strange that she couldn't sleep all night long, sure that any minute the phone would ring.

Rebecca stretched out on the floor of the hut, feeling filled by the food and tired once more.

# 2

She awoke hungrier than before, feeling as though she'd never eaten. The fruit basket had been refilled, and she picked out a fat, oozing plum. She thought she heard birds in flight, and then the call of a lone bird marking out its territory, warning away other birds; at least, that's what she'd always been told the lilting songs of birds really meant.

Before she read the second letter, she allowed herself the luxury of eating the plum first. Then she inserted her finger beneath the sealed envelope flap.

*Dear Sagana,*

*Don't you remember our first meeting, back in class 5-A? I spotted you immediately: your blonde hair in pigtails to your waist and your long unclean fingernails. You sat in the front row, scratching your neck and watching me through thick smudged eyeglasses.*

*That year I was so lovely, wasn't I, in my nine-year-old way? With my curled Toni home-permanent, my powder-blue blouse with puffed sleeves, my short navy blue flared skirt dotted with tiny white hearts? And I've been lovely ever since, haven't I?*

Rebecca stopped reading and closed her eyes, terrified suddenly, recalling the reaction of the boy who was not Howard Geller. Had this trip to the mountain destroyed her beauty?

"Ms. Nutty Narcissus Narcissist, my best friend," Sagana used to tease her.

18

"Rebecca reeks of egotism," Evan had declared once, over Chinese food.

"How," her mother used to muse when her daughter was still small, "did this one ever get such a swelled head?"

Years after the incident in the staircase, Arnie approached her, although they'd barely exchanged two words since then. Rebecca was fifteen and blooming, smug in her new knowledge that boys and men would fall at her feet. Arnie had become a pothead.

"Hey, Becky," he said, "you think you're such damned hot stuff. You didn't even know how to kiss that time. Remember who taught you!"

Rebecca returned his stoned gaze, tossing her long wavy hair back. "I'm sure I don't recall." Although of course she did recall; had, in fact, never forgotten that first thrill.

When Rebecca was seventeen, her mother felt it was necessary to talk to her. "Why do you date boy after boy, but never any steadily . . . like the other girls? And you're always with Sagana, and she hardly dates at all!"

"Because," Rebecca answered, "it's that first thrill I care about, not the boys. I have all the fun I want with Saggie, so it's just that . . . thrill . . . that special uncovering each time." She'd tilted her head to stare at her stunned, miserable, embarrassed mother. "Don't you know what I mean?"

And until Evan, that was all that counted for years: that first touch. Unveiling her body to a new man. Seeing another one fall. Each time another man said, "You're beautiful," and then broke up with the woman he'd been seeing for a year, Rebecca was happy. Perhaps best of all was telling Saggie about each conquest.

19

Rebecca looked at the letter she was still holding in her hand and resumed reading.

*Mrs. Damiano didn't seat me in the front row with you, but I watched you sometimes during those first few weeks of class 5-A. Your dirty fingernails bewildered me. You had a slight rash on your arms. When you finally invited me home for lunch, I was almost afraid to go. But you were so insistent that I succumbed.*

*Your parents' apartment was filled to capacity with paintings on the wall, knickknacks, two cats, and four unpruned philodendron plants. The apartment was ours alone, since your parents both worked and Arnie and little Miranda ate their lunches in school. We were going to play games, you told me, so there wouldn't be time for any lunch after all.*

*"I'm hungry," I said.*

*You looked at me. "No. You're stirring the pot. I walk in. Just stir a pot. And I walk in . . ."*

*I stirred an imaginary pot.*

*"Cackle!" you commanded.*

*I cackled. Once slightly, wishing I could at least have a cupcake. I cackled again, thinking I'd make the best, if I had to, of this lunch hour; but suddenly I was shrieking and chortling and dancing, and the imaginary broth I stirred seethed, bubbled, brewed. I screamed, while you danced around me, singing a song. I cackled, crowed, and sang, and when I returned to class 5-A, forty-five minutes later, I'd fallen in love.*

*But what would you have done if I hadn't responded? What if I'd run back to my mother's tuna fish and white bread? Or if I'd grown bored and switched on your parents' black and white television? Would you have taken those dirty fingernails and raked my face? I imagine you smiling a new kind of smug smile at the idea as you read this letter on the mountain and nurse the two infants— mine and yours.*

*I lost all interest in making other friends at school. I laughed at the other girls' warnings that you were crazy. I declined invitations to boy-girl parties because you weren't invited. Kissing the little boys in our school could never have equalled an afternoon of games and songs with you.*

*Faithfully,*
*Rebecca*

The fever returned. She grew hot. She thought she heard what might have been an animal screaming, and she did the only thing she could do. She slept.

# 3

Rebecca awoke and remembered the old games, the games with the imaginary shark and the games with the dolls.

She is lying in bed with Sagana. They are about ten years old, and Sagana wears a pair of lemon-colored Bermuda shorts with matching T-shirt and hair ribbon, making her look nearly jaundiced. Rebecca is in a black jumper with red roses embroidered on the bib and pockets. "He's coming," Rebecca cries. "I feel him!"

"Me too," cries Sagana. "I feel him too!"

And so, side by side on Sagana's parents' king-sized bed they lie rigidly. They cling together, waiting for the aquatic fiend, the sleek sharkie, to begin nibbling first so gently at their toes, then with more fervor at their calves and eventually biting large pieces from their thighs and stomachs.

"He's biting my throat," moans Rebecca.

"He's biting mine, too."

"Let me have the mirror, quick," Rebecca demands, since part of the game requires looking into the magnifying side of Sagana's mother's make-up mirror. Rebecca stares at her face, at her cheeks, her neck, the tops of her shoulders which are left bare by the sleeveless black jumper. "Oh, I'm so red," she moans, thinking herself the most beautiful actress of all.

"Flushed," agrees Sagana. "You're rosy red."

She thought about the dolls: the assorted tossed-aside wiggling hula dancers from the back seat of her father's car, the rubber four-inch men originally designed to hold vitamin tablets, the toy soldiers with missing arms and legs found in the schoolyard, the chewed-upon dinosaur donated by the old lady who ran the five-and-ten near school, and the two baby dolls, neither of which cried nor wet nor said Mama: Black-Haired-Bazooka-Baby whose hair had been shorn by a razor blade during the same game in which her skin had been partially dyed black, and chubby Premature Baby, missing one eye.

Most of the dolls had two names, two personalities: Heart's Joy, a pleasant and subdued Chinaman, was also the dastardly Olive Tit, owner of a gambling casino and given to dark urges; Aunt Moonlight, the maternal Hawaiian in the plastic grass skirt, was also the wild Lola Lips who emerged primarily to cater to the needs of the demanding, lustful Olive Tit.

She remembered the games:

"Olive Tit meets Bubbles in a bathtub . . ."

"Robusto snatches Bitchette's purse . . ."

"Premature Baby tries to murder Vitamin Boy, but Aunt Moonlight helps him to escape, then Vitamin Boy hunts down Premature Baby and kisses her until she falls senseless . . ."

Shyly, Sagana picks up Premature Baby, Rebecca's one-eyed diapered baby doll. Rebecca, the now savage Vitamin Boy, grabs Premature Baby, flinging her down, simulating noises of imagined passion . . .

"Premature Baby has a baby!" And they enact a birth scene, creating birth noises and birth gestures, amazed at how much more like Olive Tit than Vitamin Boy the newborn infant looks.

Next, Rebecca imagined she was back in her apartment, the apartment she shared with Sagana.

She is lying in her bed wearing a black nightgown. Suddenly a male figure is standing above her. He starts to walk away, not floating, walking quite solidly. Rebecca, still in her black nightgown, follows. He walks from the bedroom into the living room, out into the hallway of the building, down the four flights of stairs, to the street and the subway station. Rebecca continues to follow. His walk becomes increasingly familiar. As they stand side by side before the token booth, she realizes it is Evan, that it is his black slightly-mussed hair, his olive skin and classic nose, his plaid shirt and fitted corduroy Levis.

After riding several stops, they leave the train together and Rebecca follows him to his apartment. He walks inside to his bedroom. He removes his jacket, shirt, shoes, socks.

Sitting on the bed, on top of the bedspread, in his corduroy jeans, leaning against the headboard, he looks at her for the first time, although now her back is to him. She stands in front of the dresser watching him through the mirror.

Evan smiles. "Sweet, pretty Rebecca," he murmurs. "Faithful Becky. Mother of my child."

From the mirror to his bed, onto that paisley bedspread and into his arms, and his arms are the same, and his mustache feels the same, and his skin is the same.

Then Evan hands her the crumpled note which Sagana left for her on the floor by the refrigerator. She wonders why Evan has the note. And now the second half of the note, the part that Sagana had printed with a thick black magic marker, is most vivid. Rebecca hates this part of the note. She doesn't want to think about it.

REBECCA, YOU ARE TOO TIMID TO SEIZE
POWER, SO I'M TAKING YOUR DAUGHTER
AND MY DAUGHTER TO A PLACE WHERE
WOMEN WILL BE ABLE TO CREATE THE
WORLD ANEW! A NEW WORLD, A NEW RACE!
YOU—SEDUCTRESS!—DON'T DESERVE TO
COME.

# 4

The last envelope was sealed more firmly than the rest, with scotch tape along the flap, and Rebecca struggled for a moment, fearful of breaking her fingernails.

*Dear Sagana,*

*If I say I'm sorry, will that make it all better? Will you come home? I haven't said it yet, but I'll say it now: I'm sorry, I'm sorry! If I say that I will hold my little baby Lily in my arms, that I will tickle her and blow air into her tiny bellybutton, will you accept my apology? Accept my apology for what, though? I'm still unsure what crime I've committed. But Sagana, your old friend Becky will apologize anyway. But will you forgive? Perhaps if I recall the facts . . .*

Rebecca marveled at her own tone in the letter: so confident, nearly cocky. On the floor of the hut now, she was none of those things, and the letter might as well have been written by some stranger.

*A fact: men were in and out of my bedroom during the time we lived together. Everywhere, I met men. But it was merely the lust I loved, not the men; you knew that until, of course, Evan. The aloof Evan.*

*A fact: soon I was pregnant with Evan's child. And . . . another fact: you too became pregnant at the same time. The two of us? But I never questioned you. You wouldn't have let me. But something had happened. Sag-*

*gie, you too must have discovered lust . . . somewhere.*
*But I didn't want to know.*

Rebecca felt a sudden desire to stop reading. She still
didn't want to know and she never would. But she continued to read.

*Another fact: "This isn't right," I would say to you*
*over and over during our pregnancies.*
*"How dare you talk about right and wrong?" you'd*
*ask. "When we were kids and played with dolls, were we*
*right then? Shouldn't we have been arranging pizza dates*
*for Barbie and Ken dolls, rather than rape scenes be-*
*tween Olive Tit and Black-Haired-Bazooka-Baby? You*
*loved being the baby doll, the little seductress in the frilly*
*panties who was seduced by wild Olive Tit! Your skin*
*would turn rosy, your eyes would shut . . . What's so*
*right about that?"*
*"But," I kept repeating, "I don't want a baby. I'd*
*rather take out the dolls again than nurse a real infant. I*
*don't want something draining the milk, the spirit from*
*my breasts! My breasts are sensual, not mothering!"*
*And you would say, "Be quiet. Be still. Your kind of*
*love is no longer what matters. Our daughters will be*
*different." You were the Sagana in control once more.*
*Evan had vanished from my life, and the Sagana from*
*that first lunch hour had returned, fully in command. I*
*never even questioned that they would both be girls. You*
*seemed to know.*
*And why had I allowed myself to go through with it,*
*why hadn't I arranged an abortion without your knowl-*
*edge, without your consent? But I knew why. I couldn't*
*bear your anger, Sagana, I never could.*
*You took my dolls out of our big closet, out of the*

*steamer trunk in which they'd been stored, dusting them, talking to them, chatting as though to old friends. "Premature Baby," you'd laugh, "I've missed you, you silly little urchin . . ." At dinnertime I'd sit, holding back tears, not wanting to eat, disgusted by the broiled steaks and buttered vegetables you set out. When I ate, it was only because you insisted. "There's a baby inside you, Becky," and you'd rock Aunt Moonlight in your arms. "Eat."*

*At night I couldn't sleep, and I'd rock myself in my own arms and stare at the ceiling. One night I got out of bed and stood in front of the wall. I wondered whether I could destroy the baby and myself too if I stepped back and plunged, stomach first, into the hard wall. But I couldn't do it.*

In the hut, Rebecca felt ashamed. How frightened she'd been.

*Back to the facts then: we were pregnant. Evan vanished, we gave birth, you took the babies and ran off to the mountain. These are facts . . . but they're also mysteries to me.*

*And what can I say about the babies? They were noisy and needy, pooping and wetting and spitting up. The one that was mine needed me all the time: Mama, it said in every way, change me, kiss me, touch me, give me. And I couldn't, Sagana, I simply couldn't. The doctors were reassuring. "Post-delivery depression," they pronounced. "Very common."*

*Unlike the doctors, you weren't understanding. You declared me cold, inhuman. You would hold the two infants in your arms, pretending to have given birth to both of them, pretending not to hear me, never speaking to me.*

*My decision is made. Soon I'm coming to find out what exists between you and the babies that you have substituted for what existed between us. To find out if Evan is there, too. Expect me soon. I'm taking care of last minute details; getting ready, readier all the time.*

*Faithfully,*
*Rebecca*

# 5

The hut grew stifling hot; Rebecca was perspiring. She imagined that they were speaking on the telephone.

"This is me," she begins.
"I know."
"Why did you leave?"
"You know why."
"I do NOT!"
"You know why."
"Why do you hate men?" In the background she hears birds shrieking. "Why do you hate . . ." she changes the last word, "me?" The birds scream. "What on earth are those birds?"
"Those aren't birds. They're the babies."

Her fever diminished; she now sat up with no difficulty. After a few moments, she was even able to stand. Then with no hesitation, she walked out of the hut. The huge sun was blazing. She couldn't believe it was the same sun that shines on the midtown streets of New York City, and that she hadn't landed on another planet.

The foliage was lush. Her eyes were drawn to the bright green swaying leaves of the trees, but she didn't know what types of trees they were. She felt like an alien. Always, to the outdoors, to the land, Rebecca was a stranger. She'd been reared for taxi riding and bus hopping, afternoon shopping sprees, dusky cafes and late night bars. Open space frightened her.

No people. No evidence of there ever having been people. No discarded soda cans, no crushed cigarette packs. How proud she was when it occurred to her to search for footprints, but there were none: no animal prints, no human prints.

There was a noise. She shivered, embarrassed by her own terror, when suddenly from behind a tree emerged the boy who was not Howard Geller.

"Howdee," he muttered, affecting a diffident, down-home stance, shuffling his foot in the dust.

She would force herself to be civil to this brat, this New York kid pretending to be a hillbilly. No, more than that, she'd be charming. She smiled. "Hi. I was wondering if you knew where my suitcase was . . . all my things . . ."

The boy's eyes narrowed. "Hmnn . . . nope . . . don't reckon I've seen a suitcase in a coon's age . . . you mean one of them big old city-slicker valise types? Mighty sorry, Missy . . ."

Moron, she thought. She took a deep breath. "Listen," she said, "I'm a little nervous. All by myself in a strange place. All this space . . . Maybe you could walk with me for a while . . ."

He seemed to consider. "Wal, why not? Hate to see a woman-folk upset. Never can tell what critters might pop out from behind one of these big old trees and scare a woman-folk to death."

She hoped he'd soon grow tired of playing hillbilly. Silently, they began to walk together. The heat was worse, as though the whole world had come down with her fever. "Is it always this hot here?"

"Hot? You call this hot? Hoo boy . . . you'd better get a move on then, you think this is hot!"

"Look, Howard Geller, will you stop this hillbilly

business? Why don't you quit playing games?" She just couldn't be charming with this kid.

He turned sulky. "I'm not Howard Geller. Howard Geller was a junior at Dalton. I never went to Dalton."

At least he'd stopped the hillbilly accent, Rebecca thought. "Okay, Howard. Whatever you say or don't say."

"Alright, maybe I am Howard Geller. So what?"

"Nothing. After all, this is your territory, and I'm just a stranger."

For the first time, she fully realized that this was Howard's territory, not just Sagana's. So why had Sagana come to a place where there were males, if she was so set upon a world made up of women only? She stared more closely at the boy in front of her . . . definitely male.

"Now you're talking," he said.

"First off, no matter what you think, I'm going to find Sagana and Lily. I mean, she must want to see me . . . she left me a note. She must have expected me to follow! We're best friends. We have been since fifth grade. Recently she hasn't approved of certain of my . . . orientations. It's that simple."

He turned hillbilly again. "Wal, I'll level with you, since you seem like a nice enough lady, even though you are kind of sickly. Seems I do recollect a group of people—now I ain't necessarily sayin' they're the exact ones you have in mind—livin' in some huts just a wee bit down this here road you and I been travelin' along. Now, iffen that ain't a coincidence to beat the band, my name ain't not Howard Geller."

She tried to sound only slightly curious, suddenly detached. "Just a little bit more to go? Well, we might as well give it a try."

He stopped. "Sorry, little lady, here's where you and me part ways. At least for now. I've got work to do, so I'll just be a'headin' on back to the old corral." He walked away quickly into a thick group of trees, not waiting to see Rebecca's reaction.

Rebecca shook her head. She continued walking; she didn't want to waste any more time wondering who this bratty kid was, nor why he was living in Sagana's mountain commune.

Quickly she strode, aware of footprints where before there had been none. Big black flies were now buzzing near her head, crawling into her nose and eyes, and mosquitos bit her legs and arms.

The air was hot and wet. What if there were alligators and poisonous creatures with fangs? Then it occurred to her that she was on top of a mountain. Shouldn't it be cold, blustery, with fierce winds tangling her long hair?

She kept walking, trying to think about other things. About Lily. She envisioned her daughter's face, her blonde wisps of hair just growing in, her small nose with the tiny nostrils . . . At a certain point Lily had developed a rash on her scalp and the doctor had told Rebecca to rub a smelly ointment on the area three or four times a day. But she didn't like doing it, had resented it, until Sagana, of course, took over. And the diapering . . . how she'd hated that! But Sagana would bend over Lily, blowing air into her bellybutton, making her laugh so that the baby didn't squall and resist. Later, Sagana would say, "I don't know about you, Becky . . . Some day I may have to . . ." And she'd leave the statement unfinished, and only recently had Rebecca understood what she'd meant. Some day she'd leave and take the children with her and declare herself

Rebecca's enemy. But what kind of enemy left notes near the refrigerator? Just because . . . just because I like sex with men, she thought . . . just because I'm proud to be beautiful, to be attractive to men . . . just because I hadn't wanted Lily . . .

She was so hot. Perspiring, she finally allowed herself the luxury of resting. She sat beneath a tree and rested her head upon her knees. What good was her beauty in a place like this? Sagana and the other women would despise her, would rip the rings from her fingers, would pull the earrings from her ears, causing infections and deformities . . .

Without warning, it grew windy. The heat became a savage, biting cold. Her teeth began to chatter. She forced her shoulders to remain still in order to stop the chattering. Sagana had taught her that trick and sometimes it had worked for her. But not now. Chattering made one's teeth chip, very unflattering.

The trees swayed back and forth, and pieces of debris whipped past her eyes. She would have to move on; if she stayed still she'd die! What kind of place had she entered, where the weather was so cruel? Could Sagana have acquired powers which enabled her to manipulate the weather? Ridiculous.

She stood up, immediately losing her balance to a huge gust of wind. Grabbing the tree for security, she looked around her. Then she stared at her own inadequate clothes: a pair of short-shorts and sandals. She would die. She would never even have a chance to see Lily again!

A noise . . . something crackling behind her . . . Before she could turn around, two gloved hands swooped over her eyes. "Sagana? Evan?" she cried in terror, her knees giving way.

"Jesus Christ!" It was Howard Geller's voice. He removed his hands. "Sagana, Evan, Sagana! At least turn over to the flip side once in a while."

Rebecca wheeled around. Now he was dressed in a down jacket, with a brightly colored woolen ski mask pulled tightly over his face. His blue eyes shone through the eye-holes. Over his hands were thick mittens. He turned his back to her, revealing that he also wore a nylon backpack. "Open it up," he ordered, shouting over the wind. "There's a warm jacket for you, and a hat . . . and gloves . . . Come on."

She unzipped the backpack gratefully, her fingers stiff and numb. The folded-up jacket inside was identical to the one he wore. She forced her shivering arms into the sleeves. Over her head she pulled a light ski mask. The thick mittens he'd brought offered immediate comfort to her fingers. If only her legs weren't unprotected . . .

"The weather's weird around here," Howard said. "It changes all the time. And there aren't any radio d.j.s to tell you how to dress."

"Well, thank you." It was difficult to say. She was grateful he was being himself again.

"Shucks, it seemed the least I could do for a scared woman-folk who was like to freeze her buns to death. We don't need no corpses here litterin' things up . . ."

She began walking, furious that he was pretending to be a hick again. Is this what he learned at the Dalton School? She battled the wind with each step. He followed. "Listen, Howard Geller, from New York, New York, just cut this play-acting." She couldn't stop herself. She was definitely not playing the part of the charming older woman—that was certain.

He dropped the hillbilly stance and turned sulky again. "Maybe you're hallucinating. Maybe I'm just a

35

hallucination. Maybe you're still dreaming in the hut. Maybe this whole mountain is a hallucination."

Hallucination? Rebecca stared at him. Only his eyes and lips showed through the slits cut out of his ski mask. His jacket was zipped way up on his neck, nearly to his chin. He didn't look exactly human in that outfit. "You probably are a hallucination," she said, "left over from my fever. But I can go on without you, you know," she yelled, closing her eyes against flying particles of dust. "I don't need you. Sagana left me a note by the refrigerator. I'm supposed to follow! I want Lily. She doesn't even want you up here, I'm sure. She's using you for something—she'll get rid of you!"

"You're nuts."

They were standing still now, and a flurry of leaves blew into their faces. "Good-bye," Rebecca shouted. "I'll find them myself!" She took a few slow steps, annoyed that her nose was running beneath the wool mask. This could cause an ugly rash, and without any lotions it might never go away, it might leave scars . . . She felt his presence beside her before she saw him. "Howard Geller, why are you coming with me? Don't bother . . ."

"Don't tell me what to do. I do what I want." She could imagine him telling his teachers at the Dalton School exactly this.

Again they walked in silence. The wind died down as quickly as it began. Every few minutes, Rebecca expected to see a cluster of houses and people building fires, chatting, exchanging idle gossip over picket fences. But she knew that wasn't Sagana's style. Women chatting over picket fences? Women having tupperware parties?

"Are we almost there?" she asked. Her legs were hurting.

36

He shrugged. He was doing a drum riff in the air with his fingers. She decided to ignore him. A hyperactive teenager was not what she needed. They walked on. After a while, though, she couldn't stop herself from asking again whether they were almost there.

He shrugged again and this time played an imaginary guitar. He jumped up and down, gyrating like a rock star.

"I can't go on!" she finally declared, conscious, even with the cold and weariness of her body, of the melodramatic sound of her words. She liked that sound. She wondered if Howard would respond like a movie hero and take control of the situation. She hoped he would. Did sixteen-year-olds know about such things?

He did. "Shall I carry you?" His voice turned husky and virile.

She looked closely at him to see if he was making fun of her. No, he seemed to be taking his new role as hero very seriously.

"No. No, I think I can hold out a little bit longer," she answered softly. "But isn't there somewhere to rest, just for a little while?" She was comfortable in this vulnerable and coy role.

He hesitated. "I know a hut . . . it's a little out of our way . . . but it's empty . . ." Like a virile movie star he became decisive—to hell with all obstacles. "We'll do it! Come on!" He spun around, taking the lead.

And sooner than she anticipated, they came upon a tiny hut. They bent down and walked inside. The instant warmth was so miraculous that she looked around for a radiator and listened for the whine of steam surging through pipes. Without speaking, they removed their down jackets and ski masks and gloves. Rebecca's feet suddenly felt too hot. She pulled off her sandals. Her naked feet were red and slightly swollen, and she caressed them with her fingers, sighing as she did so. Howard Geller watched her.

"I'm so tired," she announced, lying down carelessly in a corner.

Hours later, when she awoke from a dreamless sleep, she found Howard asleep with his head upon her breast. She stiffened. He was just a boy. His body was so gangly. But he did have such beautiful skin. And thick long hair. And she did thrive on conquests. She craved sexual tension and intrigue, flirtation and seduction. Sagana had once called her a tool of men. A tool? No. Never.

Then she became aware of his mouth seeking her breast, seeking the nipple of her breast. Howard Geller placed his lips against the nipple, over the fabric of her blouse. His eyes remained shut as he continued to kiss her there, over and over.

Rebecca remembered Arnie in the staircase, one of her favorite memories, and she felt once more the joy of being desired. In fact, Howard was just the age that Arnie had been. "Don't worry, Howard," she crooned, stroking his hair, almost smiling. "I'll teach you . . ." And she guided his boyish hands over her breasts and along her thighs. She gasped and licked her lips, to show him his power. She moaned, a long, sensual sound. Love with a young virgin, especially one who had been resistant to her beauty at first, was really too exciting. She stared at her flushed skin and allowed her tongue to graze her shoulder. "Sagana," she whispered, "you can't win."

# 6

They slept after lovemaking, the heat of the hut keeping them warm. When they awoke she told Howard the details of Sagana's betrayal. He sat in front of her, no longer the wisecracking smartassed kid, but a respectful, misty-eyed male, listening attentively to the woman he'd so recently embraced. Rebecca felt herself truly beautiful and powerful once more: it would be easier for her from here on in. She had an ally—no, she had a conquest—better yet, maybe a disciple. She would shape this young boy at her whim. Whatever Sagana wanted him for had to be something terrible, whereas what she would ask of him would be precious and sacred. He could offer her a sexual devotion, a sensual commitment, adoration without question or demands. No harem would be necessary for her, just young, devoted Howard. Besides, she'd need a babysitter for Lily if she really intended to take her home.

They emerged from the hut, hand in hand, to find altogether different weather: a springlike, slightly breezy day with a pale, benevolent sun. Rebecca still noted the absence of any birds, surprising herself by doing so. She guessed that life outdoors was beginning to affect her. She pointed at a tree a few yards ahead of them. "What kind of tree is that?"

Howard squinted. "I don't know. The women up here run the outdoor show. They know how to do just about everything. They garden, they build fires, they cure snakebite, they trap animals for food . . . they're also terrific runners. They run for hours every day."

He sounded so impressed that she felt jealous. Could he possibly have crushes on these women? "Do they sell vanilla cookies too?" she asked maliciously.

Howard didn't laugh.

"Well, Howard, don't you ever wonder why Sagana and her self-sufficient friends want you around? And how many men are up here, anyway? Doesn't it occur to you that you should be scared?"

"How many of us are up here?" He stopped and thought for a moment. "Well, I'm the youngest. Actually, not many. Actually, only two of us. And I'm just a boy, really, don't you think? Not quite a man yet . . ." He shrugged. "Well, in some ways I'm coming along, I guess."

She couldn't believe how snotty he could be. "Did they teach you to be that snotty at the Dalton School?"

He shrugged. "And why should I be scared? There aren't any problems between the men and women here. This is a place for people tired of urban bullshit. That's all. And I already told you," now he was whining, "I don't know who this Sagana is."

Rebecca remained silent after that. Was he telling her the truth? There seemed to be no reason for him to lie to her any longer—he was going to be hers, after all.

They walked on. Soon, in the distance, she was able to distinguish numerous huts, a stream, and rising smoke. She clenched her fists. "Is that it?"

Howard nodded and began playing his imaginary guitar again. He mouthed the words to a song.

She walked more quickly. Little by little, Howard fell behind her. "What's wrong?" she demanded.

"I don't know if Sagana is here," Howard said. He was whining again.

He must drive his parents nuts, Rebecca thought. "I

thought you told me you don't even know who Sagana is!"

"I don't know what I know. And look, I'm not going to be able to come with you."

"But . . . after what we went through? Are you afraid? Think of the things I just showed you . . ."

Howard distorted his features, crossed his eyes, and then smirked. He shuffled his feet. "Wal, Missy, aintcha big and brave enough to handle this on your own?"

"You cretin!" she shouted. "You moron!"

"I told you already 'bout how high my I.Q. is. Those stupid teachers at Dalton wouldn't even tell my mother how high it was."

I will stay in control, Rebecca told herself. "Fine," she murmured icily. "Fine. Then get out of my sight."

Howard stooped over in a mocking bow, then turned around and began to walk away. He headed back the way they had come, and he never once turned around. He was doing drum riffs in the air.

She was alone again. Why had she ever come? She wanted to cry. Instead, she decided to sing in order to cheer herself up as she walked closer to the group of huts. She would compose a pretend-blues the way she and Saggie used to with the dolls in front of the full-length mirror. Saggie would hold the orange-colored rubber Vitamin Boy and give him the throaty Satchmo role, while Rebecca would grab Aunt Moonlight and transform her into Lola Lips, now a sultry singer in a plunging scarlet dress. The songs they used to sing! Together, their husky voices would merge while the two dolls bobbed in their hands.

*Oh, gimme a bottle and I'll be your dear*

(Saggie would shriek as Vitamin Boy)

*Gimme a bottle and a kick in the rear*

(Rebecca would purr as Lola Lips)

Now Rebecca tried to sing by herself, without Sagana and the dolls, but no song came to her. The muscles in her calves felt so tight that surely they would explode. Perspiration was pouring down her face when she reached the edge of what was undoubtedly a settlement, perhaps Sagana's commune.

She found herself standing on the opposite side of a narrow clear stream, across from a young blonde girl washing clothes and wearing a white dress. The girl looked no older than eighteen. Her dress reminded Rebecca of a wedding dress, with its wide skirt and dainty embroidery. She could be Howard's teenaged bride. She looked shy and innocent. Could this teenager be one of the women under Sagana's spell? An . . . Amazon? Could this girl be a warrior? Sagana must have recruited her from a castle somewhere, where she'd sat waiting for Prince Charming. How did such a tiny, ethereal creature survive a climate that did somersaults every hour? The girl didn't look up to acknowledge her. "Hi," Rebecca greeted her, not knowing what else to say.

After the slightest hesitation—so slight it possibly was imagined—the girl looked up, directly into Rebecca's eyes. Her eyes took Rebecca by surprise: although they were as blue and as pale as she'd suspected they would be, they were unexpectedly angry. She remained silent, holding Rebecca's gaze with her own.

"What's the name of this place?" asked Rebecca

softly, her heart pounding, unable to break the girl's gaze.

"The name is on the tip of your tongue," the girl said angrily in a deep voice. "All women know the name of this place. We are born knowing the name! But you're not courageous enough to speak it aloud." She bent down to gather her clothes from the stream. Her little hands reminded Rebecca of small birds. Through the sheer white fabric of her dress Rebecca could see her ribs.

"Will you help me find Sagana?" Rebecca managed to ask, watching as the girl wrung out her clothes. The girl didn't reply. She flung the clothes over her delicate arm and began to walk away, heading toward a large hut. Rebecca took a risk: "Must you be so self-righteous?" she called out after her. The girl didn't change her stride or look around.

Rebecca watched the girl in white disappear inside a large brown hut which looked taller, broader, and sturdier than the other small huts. She wondered if she'd gone inside to alert the officials of her arrival. If so, someone was, bound to come out and talk to her, whether for friendship's sake or not . . . Perhaps their Welcome Wagon would send a representative to her . . . a woman in a toga with one exposed breast offering her a bag of potato chips and creamy onion dip.

# 7

She crossed the stream, carefully hopping over a few stones, marveling at the lovely spring weather. The strong and surprising odor of baking bread wafted by. She grew ravenous. She recalled that Sagana had become an expert bread baker during her pregnancy. Often Rebecca would come home to find her engrossed in the whipping and stirring and beating of eggs and flour and sugar: banana breads, sour dough breads, date nut breads . . . For a moment she was certain that Sagana was standing in front of an oven nearby, kneading dough with those strong, capable arms. No, not Sagana, not yet; she wasn't going to make it easy for Rebecca to find her, that seemed clear. Yet it also didn't make any sense: if Saggie really hadn't wanted anything to do with her again, she would never have left the note. But then . . . why this game of hide and seek?

She chose a tree and sat down inside its shadow, stretching her legs out in front of her, wondering what Lily looked like now, wondering how much change the months away had made, and whether her little girl missed her. Had Lily even noted that one of her two mothers was gone? Why should she notice Rebecca's absence? Really, she'd never mothered her, at least not in the way that Saggie had expected. Lily had seemed distanced from her, fragile, alien. Lily might break in half, and it would be Rebecca's fault. What was the proper way to hold her, to feed her? Lily demanded too much. Rebecca hadn't felt like a woman when trying to

44

rock her to sleep, or when changing her diaper. Which wasn't the way it should be . . . All the magazines said that her womanhood would become enhanced through mothering. But she disagreed! Her breasts now sagged just the tiniest bit. She was sure she looked older. And Sagana had been so willing to assume her responsibilities, to take care of both babies. No matter what, though, she was going to remove Lily from this world of Saggie's.

Nobody emerged from the large hut that the woman in white had entered. It seemed that she had been inside a long time. Without a watch, Rebecca couldn't be sure.

It was still warm and sunny; the odor of the bread was captivating, her fever had vanished, and the stream in front of her looked so inviting. For weeks the dirt had been caking on her skin. How delightful to be clean again! To be dripping wet. Impulsively she stood and unzipped her shorts, then slid them quickly down her legs. Next she eased her shirt off and shook out her long hair. The air caressed her body. She stood with legs apart, planted firmly beneath her. Then she leaned way over to the side in one direction and then way over to the other in order to stretch, to feel her own agility, her own power. Perhaps, she thought, being so close to Sagana made her strong.

She walked to the edge of the stream and dipped in a foot. Her nipples grew tense as she splashed the cool water over her legs and thighs. Goose bumps appeared on her arms and chest. She stepped in. It wasn't deep. Carefully, she scrubbed herself.

At last, when she felt cleansed and refreshed, she relaxed and floated on her back. Her eyes closed against the hot sun. She could stay like this forever, she could happily forget her mission. She imagined her own body within the world created by her sealed eyes, imagined herself on a blonde-colored beach, nude, with someone . . . Someone seen only vaguely . . . In her fantasy only she herself, naked, was clearly delineated . . . Her strong thighs spread wide apart in the fantasy, as they spread apart in the cool water. The water teased her breasts. She imagined herself turning over, the blonde sand glistening on her skin, belly side up, breasts taut and firm, round nipples glowing in the sunlight . . .

She opened her eyes. A woman was walking briskly toward the stream. Rebecca stopped floating and hid her body beneath the water. The woman smiled. Rebecca squinted at her, trying to see her clearly against the sun. She wore nylon shorts and a tight black sleeveless shirt. What was immediately striking was how lithe and muscular she was: her thighs and calves rippled with strength. Equally striking were the high laced boots she wore, made of black leather and decorated with large red stars.

The woman was still smiling. Rebecca forced herself to stand up straight, revealing herself once again. The woman stared at her as she stepped out of the stream, dripping water. Defiantly, she forced herself to stand tall in front of the woman. Let her look at me, she thought . . . But she felt herself trembling despite her anger. She felt too vulnerable like this, too revealed somehow.

The woman was much taller than Rebecca. "I'm Rhea," she announced in a flat voice.

"Rebecca." Her voice sounded faint, even to herself. Hurriedly she turned to find her clothes. She didn't want this woman, this Rhea, to stare at her. But she was too wet to get dressed. What could she do, though, stand here naked and wait for the sun to dry her? Well, why not? Her embarrassment made her angrier. "Were you sent by the others?" she asked boldly.

Rhea didn't respond, merely allowing her eyes to slowly travel the length of Rebecca's body.

Rebecca retreated to the same tree which had sheltered her before. She sat down beneath it, awkwardly trying to shield herself from view.

Rhea spoke. "You seemed to be having quite a good time there in the stream . . ." She was not smiling anymore, and there was no trace of humor in her words.

Wet or not, Rebecca started to put on her clothes. "I . . ."

"You don't have to be embarrassed." Rhea came and sat beside Rebecca.

Rebecca stared curiously at Rhea's even-featured face. She had wide green eyes, a pert upturned nose and full, sensuous lips. She had a fashion model's face. And a man's muscular body. Rebecca noted for the first time the silver half-moon-shaped earring in her left ear. "Are you one of Sagana's women?"

At last Rhea laughed. She threw back her head and roared. She scratched her stomach, lifting up her shirt a few inches. "Well, maybe I am . . . and maybe I don't know what you're talking about," she said in a lazy drawl. Rhea's sudden drawl reminded Rebecca of Howard Geller. Did everyone here think it was cute to play hillbilly?

"Look," Rebecca pursued, "where is Sagana?" Rhea didn't seem exactly friendly, but she didn't seem hostile either.

Rhea changed the subject. "Are you hungry, Rebecca?" There was still no sympathy in her voice. Her tone was entirely objective, as though Rebecca were

47

just an object of curiosity. "I was baking bread in my hut before," she continued. "You can come by and have some."

"Thank you," Rebecca answered coldly. Of course she was hungry, desperately hungry. At the offer of food her belly tightened. But she hated being condescended to. Did Rhea think she was performing a charitable deed by offering her bread?

The two women rose and stood together. Rhea walked a few feet ahead of Rebecca over the grassy path. Her long muscular legs allowed her to maintain a pace which Rebecca couldn't match.

"I smelled the bread," Rebecca said softly after a minute or two, attempting to make conversation. "It smelled delicious." Even to her own ears, such casual chatter seemed absurd, and it bothered her to have to address Rhea's back. Rhea didn't turn around or change her pace, and at that moment something occurred to Rebecca. "Amazons didn't eat bread!" she shouted. "I just remembered that from my Classics course in college. Only meat; no bread, no vegetables!" So there, she implied, you're not the real thing!

Rhea still didn't acknowledge her.

The terrain over which they traveled was, for the most part, smooth and grassy, and the grass tickled Rebecca's ankles. At one point she stooped and removed her sandals and held them in her hand, so that she could enjoy the tickling sensation on her bare feet.

Rhea didn't slow her pace to wait. Rebecca fell even further behind. They passed a few huts which were made of what seemed to Rebecca to be stone, but she wasn't sure. Although they passed no people, she could pick out signs of their existence—wet clothes draped on rocks to dry in the sun, and the charcoal remains of small fires. There were also what looked like the remnants of meals, although she didn't want to stare too closely at any of these, imagining bits of undigested raw meat along with animal bones.

Finally, Rhea stopped before a small hut. The smell from the bread was overpowering, and she felt faint with hunger as she followed Rhea inside.

# 8

Rebecca stood awkwardly inside the cramped hut. In one corner stood a small old-fashioned oven, on top of which two plump loaves of bread were cooling off. There were two more loaves on top of a wooden table. Rebecca looked around for a chair of some sort, but there weren't any. The hut's dirt floor was layered with pebbles, leaves, and twigs. On the wall over the oven was a large glossy picture postcard. It reminded Rebecca of the postcards sold in New York shops specializing in campy, fashionably out-of-date items. The card showed a chubby woman with black wavy hair and full red lips holding a fat cigar in her hand and blowing heart-shaped smoke rings from her mouth. Rebecca spotted another postcard on the wall on the other side of the hut: another chubby woman with ivory skin and the same black wavy hair holding a bunch of thick, purple grapes in one hand and a pack of slim exotic cigarettes in the other.

"Help yourself." Rhea pointed to the bread cooling on the table.

Rebecca walked slowly toward the table. She didn't want to feel too grateful to Rhea. The bread was spongy and warm and sweet. She felt as though she were biting into someone's flesh.

Rebecca watched as Rhea knelt down in the corner near the oven and, with a brisk one-armed movement, lifted up a wooden pitcher which Rebecca hadn't noticed before. At the same moment she spotted, also for the first time, a pile of weights—barbells and dumbbells, she guessed—on the dirt floor. Rhea handed the pitcher to her. She drank thirstily. The liquid tasted like warm fruit juice of some kind.

"Have a seat," commanded Rhea. She sat herself down on the dirt floor, then waited, stiffly and formally, for her guest to join her.

Rebecca sat awkwardly, arranging her legs in front of her. She kept one untouched loaf of bread on her lap in case she grew hungry once more.

Rhea smiled again, the same incongruous smile she'd worn earlier. She hugged her knees to her chest, and the firm muscles in both her arms and thighs bulged. "Tell me, Rebecca, why you've come here," she said.

Rebecca hesitated, then ripped nervously with her fingers into the loaf of bread. Piece after piece of bread came away in her fingers. Then she molded each piece into a round ball. "I came here," she finally responded, "to find Sagana and Lily."

"Why would you want to do that?" Rhea nodded slightly, showing no emotion.

"Because Sagana took my child from me without my consent. And because Sagana is my closest friend and . . . At least, she'd always been my closest friend. But things have gotten so strange. I thought she and I had an understanding, you know, like married couples: yes, we were different, and yes, we had different needs and expectations and desires, but that such things would never interfere . . ." She stopped speaking, wondering if she'd already said too much.

"But why? Your answers are superficial."

Rebecca felt exasperated. She stared at the postcard of the woman with the bunch of grapes and the exotic cigarettes and then back at Rhea. "Because I want to understand. And because I want Lily back. She's my child!" She stopped herself from admitting her other reasons. She wanted a chance to defend herself. Sagana had convicted her of unnamed crimes and she deserved a chance to clear her name. Also, she missed Sagana. They'd had so much fun together. She was lonely. "You see, I probably could have had Sagana arrested for kidnapping or something like that, but I didn't . . . She knew that I wouldn't . . . She was banking on that when she left me the note. And she knew, too, that although I would be hurt by her betrayal, I would also be relieved in a way, since I'd always viewed Lily as a burden. I hadn't really wanted to give birth. I'm not the mothering type, as you can see." Rhea nodded, and Rebecca grew angry at herself for this flirtatious remark, which called attention to her slender figure, her unlined face. Why in the world would she want to flirt with this woman? "Anyway, I'm curious about something . . . this silly boy, Howard Geller, why is he here?"

She waited for Rhea to comment, but there was only the same noncommittal silence, so she continued. "Okay, forget Howard Geller. There's something terrifying to me about Sagana's reaction. Things about me that she'd always accepted before triggered off all this wrath once we were pregnant. Does pregnancy have to shatter one's universe? I'd always liked having sex with men, abandoned sex, wild sex, and I'm not ashamed!" Again, she waited for some reaction, but Rhea seemed unmoved. "I'd never pursued a career or anything. My career was in kind of a seduction-area, you might say. So why Sagana's sudden fury? And that note . . . saying that for a long time she'd been meeting with a group of women and that she'd brought them here . . . to this place." She shook her head with a disbelief that still refused to completely fade, despite the reality of her surroundings.

"And are you so sure that Sagana was the leader?" At last Rhea broke her silence.

"What do you mean?" Rebecca was pleased that Rhea was acknowledging that Sagana did exist and that she was on the mountain.

"What I mean," Rhea seemed to be making an effort now to stay unemotional, "is that you seem to be assuming that we followed Sagana here. That's all."

"Look, I've got no vested interest in whether she's the leader or not, but the note by the refrigerator implied that she was coming here to found a contemporary community of . . . Amazons." Without meaning to, she giggled at the word. Immediately she regretted her mistake.

In a split second Rhea's smile turned itself off entirely. "Rebecca, the fact that the term so amuses you only manifests your own weakness, your own inability to be a real woman!" "You see," Rhea said flatly, "in a sense, Sagana *is* our 'leader,' in that it was her idea for us to leave the city and come here, and she located this land."

"Then in what sense isn't she the leader?" Rebecca was excited now. Leaning forward, she rubbed one of the round balls of bread between her fingers.

"Some of us may question certain aspects of her personality, that's all. She's a powerful lady, a dynamite woman, no doubt about that. And she's most definitely, at the present time, the strongest person here . . ."

"Your queen, your Hippolyta . . ." breathed Rebecca eagerly, pleased that the bits of information from her Classics course were coming back to her.

Rhea looked at her oddly. "If you will . . . But what

53

we don't understand is you. Her attachment to you. Why would she leave you a note? Such an action might be viewed as extremely dangerous. Also, her devotion to your daughter . . ."

Rebecca sensed that she was being blamed for something, but she wasn't quite sure what. Once again, she was being judged guilty.

Rhea fingered her silver earring. "Amazons—giggle all you want, but you only reveal your shallowness—are glad to bring daughters into the world. But not to nurse and mother them in the conventional fashion. Not to raise them to wait on men and to fear their own strength and intelligence. The children we'll raise here will be the truest women in the world. The kind of women I've always wanted to meet. Amazons didn't suckle their daughters. They brought them up on mare's milk. You seem to have so many tidbits at your fingertips, you may also recall that Amazons were rumored to possess magic horse blood in their veins . . ."

"By the standards you've erected for yourselves," Rebecca said haughtily, "I'm the better Amazon!" She had no desire to giggle at the word now. "You may all view me as being totally screwed up, but I was the one who didn't want to raise Lily like a typical mommy, I was the one who demanded my freedom . . ."

"It's not at all the same," Rhea replied impatiently.

"Well, why not? And just how many of you are there?"

"Over a dozen now. Many more in the near future," she answered. Then abruptly, "I want to tell you about myself. First about my life in New York. I was a social worker. I worked in an office in the World Trade Center. All day long I pushed paper around on my desk, and sometimes I pasted things on the wall or made some phone calls. I answered Sagana's notice in the paper: 'WOMAN SEEKING LIKE-MINDED WOMEN TO MEET ONE EVENING A WEEK TO DISCUSS RURAL LIVING.' That was all. But I was ripe and ready and not the only one. Seven women contacted Sagana in one week."

"You must have met on Wednesday evenings! She told me that she took a yoga class." Rebecca took a deep breath. How cunning Sagana had been.

"I know." Rhea looked at her sharply, as if reprimanding her for interrupting. "We'd meet on Wednesday evenings from six to nine-thirty. At first we met in an Indian restaurant. We drank a lot of Indian beer. Later, we alternated meeting in each of our apartments. Except for Sagana's apartment, since she said that she didn't want her roommate, Rebecca, to find out. Could cause certain complications, might get too sticky, she insisted. And also one woman named Mara who didn't want her husband and son to know. The rest of us were free, and we lived for our Wednesday meetings. We'd spend hours putting out wine and cheese and preparing food. The first few months we'd all just sit around and bitch and complain. The anger we each let fly. But never toward one another, and soon the common theme of our fury emerged: men! Male domination. Each of us was allowed one month of meetings in which she would be the main topic. Wonderfully cathartic. And Sagana would sit back, taking notes. Eventually, other women joined us. We savored the time together. And then Sagana got pregnant. That took us by surprise, to put it mildly. I felt betrayed. But then she brought up her original idea. We would go to some idyllic rural place that she would locate for us. It took her a

few months to find this mountain and to arrange things.
Then we waited a little longer to really discover
whether we were 'women enough,' as the saying goes. I
never doubted myself, especially since the voices were
already beginning inside my head, even back then. I
didn't know who the voices were then."

"What voices?" Rebecca couldn't decide whether
Rhea was serious or just trying to unnerve her.

Rhea laughed. "I'll get back to the voices later. Anyway, only one woman chickened out. The rest of us
came. In the meantime, Sagana gave birth. And so did
her roommate, the mysterious Rebecca. And we were
all to vanish without a trace from our city lives. No ties.
No farewell parties. Nobody to come hunting us down.
We all agreed. But then our illustrious leader herself
leaves a careless note by her refrigerator. She says she
meant to throw it out. It's peculiar . . . But I was going
to tell you all about me, Rebecca. I'm a physical fitness
buff. I've always been. After work each day, I'd still
always find time to work out. Would you like to feel
any of my muscles? But don't touch my biceps, touch
the less obvious ones, so that I don't seem like some
brute at the beach trying to impress the girls. Why don't
you touch my strong, firm inner thigh? There, that's a
good girl . . ." Firmly she guided Rebecca's fingers. Rebecca tried to pull away, but Rhea held on with a grip
of steel. "Relax, Rebecca. Just sit like that, steady your
fingers, there, that's right. Aren't I strong and firm? I
swim and run and lift weights. I used to work out at the
Y, but now I can do it all here for free in our idyllic
world, without burly men cutting corners around me on
the track and in the pool. I swim in the cool river and I
run up and down the mountain paths, and I've brought
my weights right here into the cooking hut."

"The cooking hut?"

"Yes. My job this month is to be the cook, and I've brought my weights along, so that I can work out while I'm waiting for things to sizzle, to get red hot. I sleep in my own hut. Soon, Rebecca, you're going to get a chance to visit my hut . . . As you can see, I'm very strong, and very capable of getting what I want. Those are my weights there." She pointed. "Some people get excited by their dollies, some people by their weights, and some poor souls by things we can't even discuss publicly, am I right?" Her laugh was hollow and humorless, and she poked Rebecca in the ribs with her elbow. "Would you care to see what I can do?" Without waiting for affirmation, she bounded up, at last letting go of Rebecca's fingers.

Rebecca watched nervously as Rhea screwed two of the largest metal disks to the iron bar. Rhea stood straight and proud, inhaling deeply, exhaling slowly, inhaling again. Slowly, she bent from her knees, then grabbed the bar. Breathing and grunting, obviously pleased with herself, she lifted the weights. Rhea held the iron bar at waist level, slowly lifted it to chest level, then shoulder level. She eyed Rebecca throughout. Finally, with maximum effort, she held the weights over her head. Her chest was heaving. She brought the weights down. Perspiration poured from her face onto her shirt. Her bulging arms glistened. When she bent down to place the weights to rest upon the floor, muscles in her thighs bulged. Rebecca watched in amazement.

Rhea lifted the bottom of her shirt with her hand in order to wipe the sweat from her face. She sat down in the corner of the hut. "Come here, Rebecca. Kneel down and grab my ankles. That's right." Rebecca's hands closed around Rhea's ankles. She imagined each ankle a slender human neck that she would love to strangle. "Now I'll show you my sit-ups." Rhea lay back, placed her arms beneath her head, and up and down she went, elbows to knees, back to floor, sweating, panting. Rebecca herself had sometimes done sit-ups to maintain her flat stomach, but never with such intensity. Rhea's shirt moved up and down with her, offering Rebecca an occasional glimpse of her small breasts. She counted her sit-ups noiselessly. "Sixty," she said at last, victoriously pulling away. "I could easily do sixty more."

"I'm sure you could." Rebecca wiped perspiration from her brow. She was frightened that all this activity might bring back her fever.

Rhea patted her own belly. "So now you see how strong and able I am. A wonderful specimen, an example of what a woman can be if she sets her mind to it. I'm special, Rebecca, you must be aware of that by now. And people recognize it. Perhaps your Sagana doesn't recognize it enough, but others do. In fact, others have contacted me."

Rebecca moved away. The new light entering Rhea's eyes scared her.

"As I say, others recognize my worth, my strength, my power. I can hear them. They compliment me and advise me. They're with me all day long. They're women, of course, women from another time and place. Those very women whose name made you giggle like a nervous ninny before! They know that I should be the one in command up here, that there are things I can offer that Sagana never can. They assure me that although there are many ways to gain command, the easiest, the most enticing way is sitting right beside me. They assure me that through the lovely Rebecca and her little Lily, I will get at Sagana and conquer her. Do you understand what I'm saying?"

Rebecca trembled. "Yes, I understand what you're saying." She still couldn't be sure if Rhea believed in the voices.

"I want to be your friend, Rebecca. I can understand you and aid you in ways that Sagana never could. Remember how strong I am. What I intend to do, you see, is to enlist your help in becoming the leader."

"No thanks. Sorry."

"I wouldn't dream of forcing you, Rebecca. That's not my style. And I certainly never beg. What we're discussing is a simple pragmatic barter. You do what I want, I'll do what you want. Scratching our mutual itches."

"What do I want that badly?"

"You want Lily! I can bring her to you. I can show you how to get back to New York safely with Lily in your arms. Otherwise you'll never get out of here, you'll never see your child again. If you think that I'm exaggerating, just remember your myths, Rebecca: we women warriors are Dionysian, we rip living things apart limb by limb . . ."

"Dionysius was a man! You're hypocrites, then, worshipping a man!"

"We're not so certain of his maleness," Rhea answered coldly. "His was a female heart; we suspect that the body was, as well, a guarded secret. Rebecca, really, such a little thing I'm asking of you in exchange for so much that you want."

"I couldn't," she breathed. This was absurd. Sagana wouldn't hurt her, she never would.

"Yes. You can." Rhea grabbed Rebecca by the shoulder; her fingers dug into the soft, pliant flesh.

59

"Your own voices—surely you have voices of your own—insist upon it. Such a small price to pay. And if you don't agree to do it willingly, perhaps I will go against your wishes, do things to harm you. I can do quite a bit here to harm you."

Rebecca's shoulder hurt beneath Rhea's fervent grip. What did it matter, really? Lily. She wanted Lily. And so she nodded once, eyes averted.

"How nice," said Rhea. "All of us agree that you're doing the right thing."

# 9

This time Rhea didn't walk in front of Rebecca. Now she held Rebecca's arm tightly, asserting her dominance. Rhea was so strong that Rebecca worried about black and blue marks.

Rhea's hut wasn't far. The walk there was over before Rebecca could get her bearings. Her sense of direction was poor, since she'd always survived by memorizing bus routes, hailing cabs, and letting men drive her around the city. Now she didn't know whether they were retracing steps already taken or venturing into new territory. The walk took them past no other huts, no other people. Rebecca missed the crowds and the stores of the city's streets.

Rhea gently pushed Rebecca inside the hut. She lit a candle, illuminating a large interior. A mat seemed to serve as a bed, and an Indian bedspread covered half of the mat. Another Indian bedspread, a green flowered print similar to the fabric of a dress which Rebecca had once owned, hung on the wall. Next to a camel-skin lamp, which remained unlit, was an antique baby doll. It was the kind of doll that sold for exorbitant prices, except that this doll was filthy. It wore a white soiled ripped nightie and a funny tilted nightcap. Its faded blue eyes appeared crossed and its bright red lips were now pale pink. Its cheeks were brightly and sloppily colored; Rebecca suspected lipstick or crayon. One arm was missing. The doll looked perfectly mad.

"Do you like my baby doll, Rebecca? She represents, to me, the eternal innocent in all women."

"Innocent? Then why the harlot's rouge on the cheeks?"

"To express her vibrant sexual side, of course. You can't have one without the other. Each of us brought dolls with us. Sagana's idea. We use the dolls, you see. We all chose our dolls carefully. They symbolize ourselves. I view myself as innocent and pure, Rebecca, a child growing up in a new world, one without a patriarchy. But I'm also a very sensual woman." Rhea picked up the doll and rocked it in her arms.

"Did the men have to bring dolls with them, too? Did Howard Geller bring a doll? What kind?" How did Howard fit into all this? It was driving her crazy not to know.

"You keep mentioning Howard Geller. Well, he's like our mascot. A little boy who has his purpose. I'm not fond of him, personally. Sagana wanted a couple of men up here when we first began our work. She had her reasons, and we all agreed. They don't get in our way. And they won't be here forever."

"But how in the world were they convinced to come? Why would they want to be around Amazons?"

Rhea sat down, then invited Rebecca to come and sit with her on the mat. Although Rebecca cringed, she obeyed. Rhea placed her free hand on Rebecca's thigh, still holding the doll with the other. The doll's faded blue eyes stared at Rebecca. "They didn't need to be convinced. They wanted to. They saw it as a chance to do a whole Adam and Eve thing, but to do it right this time. They were romantics. They were idealists."

So bratty Howard was an idealist. That explained why he loved playing the hero and the fool. "But that's not what you want, is it?" Rebecca asked. "Adam and Eve, Part Two?"

"Certainly not. No way. But they didn't exactly know what we women wanted. Maybe we weren't perfectly honest with them."

"But why not? And are there really only two?"

"Not anymore. And maybe less, soon." She laughed her hollow laugh.

"Evan? Is he here?"

"Evan." Rhea assumed a somber air, but her melodrama gave her away. She increased the pressure of her hand just slightly upon Rebecca's thigh. "Evan. Dear Evan." She sighed. "Evan has passed on. Just today, in fact. He's dead, Rebecca. I suppose someone had to tell you."

"Dead? How?" But as soon as she said it, she realized that she didn't want to know. This trip to the mountain was becoming a nightmare. Evan, dead?

"Yes, Rebecca. I'm sorry to have to be the one to tell you. He was thrown by a horse. He was out riding. We were all so stunned. Pandora is usually such a gentle horse. She's one of Sagana's very favorites. Thrown headfirst. Killed instantly."

Rebecca sensed how absolutely delighted Rhea was to be the first to tell her. Rebecca refused to break down and cry. Rhea would love to see her humbled even more, red-faced and hideous. She felt like smashing Rhea's doll. But she wouldn't do that either. Evan. Dead. Why had Evan come here, anyway? He was no idealist. He was . . . He had . . . No matter. No need to remember. Never. He was dead. He had betrayed her! But he was dead now. Death was ugly.

She recalled seeing death for the first time when she was eleven. She and Sagana discovered a dead man in Sagana's building. They understood at once that he'd been beaten brutally; there was so much blood—some

63

dark and clotted, some more vibrant—on the stairs where they found him. They were on their way to play with the dolls. They loved playing inside the staircase, in the dark gloomy air, underneath the sign that read "Fallout Shelter." Rebecca held Bubbles, the sweet little Dutchwoman with the bobbing head and the wooden shoes, and Sagana carried the precious Premature Baby by the legs. They both stopped short. A man in a herringbone suit lay sprawled on the fourth landing: blood poured from his mouth, his nose, his forehead. Luckily his eyes were closed, or Rebecca surely would have fainted. That was death up close, tangible death. Sagana wanted to investigate, to open his shirt, to pull down his fly, to see what happens to a male corpse, but Rebecca grew hysterical, screaming and crying. Neighbors heard her and ran from their apartments. Sagana, she recalled now, had been quiet and sullen. Later she threw a tantrum, furious at Rebecca for interfering with her investigation. So perhaps Sagana's desire had come true at last, and she'd been able to investigate . . . with Evan.

"You're so sad," said Rhea, massaging Rebecca's thigh. "How touching. But for Evan? He doesn't deserve it."

Rebecca didn't reply. Her sorrow, like her anger, was hers alone. Rhea couldn't touch it.

"Horses are strange beasts," Rhea said suddenly, almost casually. "Erratic. Powerful. Later you'll have the chance to see a very special horse. Mine. But that can wait."

"Oh? Where do you keep your horse?" asked Rebecca dreamily. Really, she didn't care. She was hardly even listening. But she hoped by chatting casually to forestall whatever it was Rhea was planning. Also, it

64

might put the sight of Evan out of her mind. "What kind is it? I don't know anything about horses, just the names of a few from an old folk song that Saggie and I used to sing: pintos and bays . . . I forget the others . . ."

Rhea took hold of one of Rebecca's arms, lifting it high, then abruptly letting go. Limply it fell back to her side. Rhea sneered. "So weak. Marshmallow. Pancake. All you pretty little glamour girls, so much time on manicures and pedicures, you neglect what's important. The first thing I've got to do is make you strong and firm, solid and indispensable to me. Get up."

Frightened, Rebecca obeyed.

"First," said Rhea, hands on her hips, "lift your arms way way up in homage to those women in heaven, get them up there, straighten those flimsy arms, that's right, now stretch, count to thirty, now stretch down, touch your toes, now to the side one way, then the other, bend more! Can't you bend?"

Rebecca continued to obey the commands barked at her. She felt as though she were in a trance. There was no hut, no mountain, no Lily, no Sagana, no dead ex-lovers thrown from the backs of horses, no insane woman communicating with internal voices, only Mrs. Mathers, her high school gym teacher, back in the large sterile high school gymnasium. Yes, Mrs. Mathers, she closed her eyes, yes, I'll bend, I'll sway, I'll jump on command. But the minutes were going by, the voice didn't stop. Mrs. Mathers never went on for so long, she had mercy. Besides, the bell surely would ring, but now this voice continued, wilder with each passing minute, with each new command. "Now the push-ups! We'll both do twenty push-ups, you're not pushing hard enough, harder!"

Silently, wearily, Rebecca knelt down and pushed

herself up and down, up and down, supporting herself with her sore arms.

"Now jumping jacks together! Follow me!"

Rebecca jumped. Her hands smarted as she clapped in time.

"Sit-ups, don't bend your knees, not ten sit-ups, fifty sit-ups, like me, a hundred sit-ups, like me, don't groan, we're both young, healthy, keep pace with me, don't stop!"

Rebecca strained, her stomach muscles aching, tense. She couldn't keep pretending this was high school. She sat up. No more sit-ups.

Rhea sat next to her, sweat pouring down her face. "Now, the weights! The finale!" Rhea bounded up toward the corner, and pulled out some more weights. These looked bigger than the ones in the cooking hut.

"No," Rebecca protested weakly, her voice a babyish whimper.

Rhea was shouting. "Now the weights! And when we're done with our exercises, we're allowed to relax, to enjoy the fruits of our flesh, to be rewarded for our hard work. But not yet. Not for hours. Work before play."

Hours more! At least an hour of this brutal exercising must have passed already. She would die before this was all over. Wearily, she stood, then fell. "Get up!" Rhea cried. "Up, up!"

Slowly she righted herself with difficulty. Things were blurring. She teetered, then managed to find strength enough to walk over to the corner and join the sweating, flushed Rhea. Rhea's tank top was soaked through, as were her shorts. Her thighs and arms glistened. Sweat rolled down her neck, her hair was matted to her face. "Up, up! Rebecca, watch me, watch me as I lift and bend and lift and bend again. You must memorize, because soon, very soon, you'll be doing the same."

Rebecca watched, forcing herself to keep her eyes open. Up and down. Rhea grunted, swayed, lifted black metal. Barbells. Dumbbells.

Rhea swayed under the weight of the objects she held. Rebecca, only a few feet away, swayed back and forth with her, weak and dizzy. She might faint, she might become ill, but she had to stand, had to watch, had to applaud, since Rhea demanded an appreciative audience. "Aren't I strong, Rebecca? Look!" Was this some kind of bizarre mating dance, a courtship ritual? "Soon, your turn!" cried Rhea.

But that was impossible! Surely Rhea must see that she was on the verge of collapse, that she wouldn't live through ten minutes' worth of weight lifting. She had never even seen weights up close until now. How insane could Rhea be, expecting her to join in this madness? If only Rhea would drop one of the weights on her toe, on her fingers, if only she would fall down and drop dead before Rebecca's eyes . . . But that wasn't likely. Although now that she squinted and cleared her wavering vision and looked carefully, very carefully, it was evident that Rhea, yes, even Rhea, was tiring! Maybe if she flattered Rhea . . . Girlishly, she clapped her sore hands. "Why, Rhea," she gushed, "you look so strong each time you bend down! More, do more!"

Rhea, holding her weights aloft in each hand, was surprised. "You like this?" she asked again, in a new seductive voice. "You like this?"

"Why Rhea, I certainly do! Please do more. I'm enchanted." Please die, she thought. Die.

"Just watch this!" shouted Rhea. "Watch what I can do!" Quickening her pace, up and down even faster,

faster than before, knees bent and then straight, arms up and then out and then in front and then down.

"Rhea, you are the very, very best!" declared Rebecca as Rhea dropped the weights on the floor, staggered a bit and then collapsed on the floor of the hut.

Rhea lay with her face down. Rebecca didn't move; she hardly breathed. Perhaps Rhea was faking. Or perhaps she had really died. Was Rebecca's will that strong?

Rhea pulled herself to a sitting position. So Rebecca was not a murderer, after all, but now she trembled in fear that she was about to be commanded to perform the weight-lifting ritual. What choice would she have but to kick this crazy woman in her teeth? She became aware that Rhea was slowly, with difficulty, lifting her shirt, sliding it upwards along her chest. Rebecca held her breath. What now? Rhea flung the shirt a few feet away; she sat, legs spread in front of her, nude from the waist up, facing Rebecca. Her ribs were clearly defined, her small breasts were more nipple than rounded flesh. They dripped sweat. Still seated, she turned around. Tattooed on her back was a black stallion. A black beast with flaring nostrils, one leg lifted haughtily. Rebecca thought once more of Evan and his fatal plunge from a horse . . . Was this some kind of veiled threat?

"Rebecca," purred Rhea. "Stroke it."

Rebecca didn't move.

"Stroke it." Rhea eased herself down so that her belly touched the floor.

Shivering, Rebecca came forward and held her hand above the horse. Her teeth began to chatter.

"That's good," spoke the prone Rhea, her voice muffled in the earthen floor.

Tentatively Rebecca touched the horse. Rhea stiffened, then sighed. Rebecca gently caressed the horse's mane, then traced her fingers around its eyes, around its wide bursting nostrils, along its elegant back, its firm haunches, she traced each leg, then over and over she allowed her fingers to follow the outline of the one leg lifted so high . . . It really was a beautiful horse. Rhea must have been brave, Rebecca thought, to have endured the pain of being tattooed. Rhea sighed again. A minute later her breathing began to come regularly, a pleasant pattern, the light breathing of someone asleep.

Rebecca continued to stroke the horse, almost expecting to hear its neigh or its whinny, to watch it leap up from Rhea's flesh, hooves flying. If only it would, she would ride off on it, allow it to carry her to Lily! The horse seemed more alive now than Rhea, as she gently stroked and caressed. Such a long time had elapsed. She fought off the urge to lie down with her head on the horse, on Rhea. She couldn't afford to be drawn to Rhea. She had to force herself instead to stand quietly. She had to steal noiselessly from the hut, to slip away from Rhea.

She stood. And waited. Rhea didn't move. Her breathing remained regular.

Rebecca looked around the hut. She grabbed Rhea's doll and then she tiptoed outside. It was nighttime. She couldn't see a thing.

# 10

Why had she taken the doll? She was tempted to toss it away. Instead, she held onto it tightly. No matter what, she had to get moving in case Rhea awoke. That was the most important thing. But it was too dark to see whether there was a path to follow, whether there was a ditch into which she might fall, whether there were objects jutting out to trip her up. Besides, her legs were sore.

Perhaps it was safest just to stay put, just to sit down right here and wait for morning's light. Perhaps that was wisest. She felt along the ground to make certain that there wasn't anything hard or cold or slimy. Then, on what felt like solid dirt, she sat.

The breeze was warm. She held the doll in her arms, wondering whether Lily had ever played with this doll. Was Lily capable of actually picking up an object of this size? What *did* babies do? Rebecca rocked the baby doll in her arms. "Baby," she whispered, something she'd never whispered to her own daughter, "baby . . ." She continued to cradle the doll, whispering her song. She was so tired. Rhea had worn her out. Soon her head drifted forward onto the doll's stomach and she fell asleep.

A noise woke her. She clutched the doll tightly. That same noise again: a crackle . . . Rhea? A horse about to step down on her head cracking her fragile skull . . .

Frightened, she turned her head to look behind her. She saw nothing. And now, straining, she heard nothing.

The brief sleep had only tired her more. What she needed was a loving massage, the kind that Saggie used to give her years ago: oil rubbed in and Saggie's firm hands gently kneading all over her body. How her muscles longed for that now. She leaned forward and was about to close her eyes once more.

At that, a figure appeared in front of her: Howard Geller in a green sweatsuit. He placed his fingers to his lips. The sweatsuit was wrinkled and dirty and he was out of breath, as though he'd been running through mud.

"What are you doing here?" she asked. He looked so young and scared himself that she didn't feel fearful.

"I'm freaked out." He closed his eyes. Then he opened them wide and spoke in a loud stage whisper. "Besides, what are you doing here? And what's with Rhea's doll?"

She didn't have to tell him anything. Why should she trust this bratty kid? She refused to care about him. Look what happened to her when she cared about people; she'd cared about Sagana and Evan and they'd both betrayed her. She had to protect herself. "Where's Evan?" she asked. Maybe Rhea had lied. Maybe he was still alive. Maybe he'd never even followed Saggie to the mountain, and her hunch about that had been wrong all along.

He stared at her. "Evan's dead."

"Oh." So Rhea hadn't lied. She sighed. She didn't want to think about Evan's death.

"Your friend Evan's dead, and boy, did I screw up again. I'd rather be back at Dalton than hanging around here."

"So now you're admitting that you know Evan. Before you said you'd never heard of him."

"I'm only sixteen. I'm just a kid. What do I know?"

"I don't care how old you are," Rebecca said, thinking that if he dared to play the hillbilly again she'd kill him. Then Saggie could investigate his death, too. It was a horrible thought. He was just a boy.

"Listen, I don't really get everything that's going on. All I know is that Sagana wanted me to take care of you in the hut when you were sick, so I did." He shrugged. "One night she came to visit me. None of the other women were with her. She said that as soon as you were better I was to bring you to her. The next night Rhea came alone and she said that if I cared at all about the common good I should bring you to her. And then she left and Mara, who always dresses in white, came, and she told me to rid the mountain of you entirely, to take drastic measures!"

So they'd all known all along that she was here. She felt bitter. "Well, you really did screw up then. You didn't take me to Saggie, you didn't take me to Rhea, and you didn't take drastic measures. You just set me loose."

He nodded. "I never do the right thing. I even failed chemistry and history in one year. And I never have any fun."

"You made love to me. Some people would think you'd done alright for yourself there."

He blushed.

"Howard, you really are just a kid, aren't you? Why did you ever come here?"

He sighed. "I hated school. I hated my parents. I didn't have a girlfriend. The other kids thought I was weird. And I liked to read the personal ads in all the papers. One day I answered one. It was easy. It was fun." He shrugged. "All I wanted was to have some fun

72

before I got too old like my parents. The ad read: YOUNG HEALTHY MEN NEEDED TO JOIN BEAUTIFUL WOMEN IN A RURAL DREAM. A GARDEN OF EDEN AWAITS YOU. ADAMS, COME MEET YOUR EVES! What could be more fun than the Garden of Eden? But now I'm running away again. I don't believe their story about Evan! He never went horseback riding. I'd rather go back and take chemistry again than let Sagana do what she did to Evan to me."

"Oh come on. You can't be saying that Saggie killed Evan? That's too crazy. Even I don't buy that." She picked up Rhea's baby doll and held it against her lips.

"Rebecca, three women up here are pregnant by Evan. Including Rhea."

"That's impossible!"

"It's true. She is pregnant. And so is Mara, and so is Lorna."

Rebecca smirked into the doll's back, which she still held against her mouth. The doll was her weapon against Howard's words. He could say whatever he wished, could try to frighten her and win her over, but it was no use. The doll's strength would protect her. With the doll, she couldn't be touched.

"You don't believe me, do you?" He started to play his imaginary guitar again, but more nervously than before. "I'll show you something that will prove to you that I'm telling the truth. Come on." He stood up. "Come on. Get up."

She stood. Why not? She'd rather be with him than all alone. Rhea might wake up any minute. "Let's go," she said to the doll.

# II

She insisted that Howard walk ahead of her. She wanted to follow behind. She still didn't trust him.

He was walking very slowly, but he didn't even turn around once to glance at Rebecca and the baby doll, to make certain that they were following. She took tiny baby-sized steps. From high above, they might have looked like children first learning to walk.

What could he offer her, she wondered. He'd already shown her once just how much he could be counted on. Once she'd hoped to make him hers alone. Now all she had left was this grinning doll who had no choice but to stay by her side.

He began to walk faster. But she continued to walk slowly. The moon had come up. It outlined him so vividly that the green of his runner's suit never faded. There was a permanent green blotch in the distance. It would be impossible for her to get lost.

She trailed the one-armed doll behind her, holding it with one hand. She felt dazed, as if she were walking within a dream. Once before she'd dreamed an evening walk . . . a walk that had led her to Evan's arms, to Evan's bed. And where would this walk lead? Evan's arms were lifeless now. Whose arms might welcome her at the end of this journey? It had better not be Rhea's bulging, maniacal grip.

Howard still hadn't turned around. Had he already forgotten her? Certainly he couldn't hear her. The distance between them muffled her tiny steps. Howard, the thwarted youthful Adam who'd naively answered an

74

ad in the newspaper. Those ads had always seemed such pitiful jokes to her, not even worth laughing at. Ads like SINGLE WHITE FEMALE, LONELY, SEEKING PROFESSIONAL MAN, 40-50, NON-SMOKER, SCORPIO OR CANCER, FOR FUN-FILLED CULTURAL EVENINGS . . . POSSIBLE LONG-TERM RELATIONSHIP. PHOTO PLEASE.

The idea that she, Rebecca, might have ever been tempted by one of those! Those five and six line appeals from such lonely people. Her body and her face had been the only advertisements she'd ever needed to draw people to her. *True, but what good,* a newly cynical voice within her questioned, *did your lovely face and your lovely body do for you? Look at you now!*

Angrily, she thrust the voice aside. She disengaged herself from it. Instead, she concentrated on her careful little steps, so delicate, her waltzing, mincing movements.

They'd begun climbing uphill. Her legs began to hurt again. How far had they traveled? Which way? To her, all ways seemed to lead in circles these days. Perhaps he was hoping to wear her out by playing an elaborate game of follow the leader . . .

The path she was climbing grew narrower, more difficult to manage, so that she was forced to clutch the doll tightly in front of her with one hand, while using her other hand for balance.

She stopped. In front of her, directly in her path, was an object. An object that seemed alive. She merely stared, unable to move, until it acquired a distinct shape. A large black bird. It was dead. A wide wing spread, a pointed black beak poised open forever as though it were about to utter an eerie death shriek. This bird . . . it was prompting something . . . that

75

memory again. No, there was no memory. Nothing had ever happened to remember. But why had Howard just left it for her to encounter? Why hadn't he moved it out of her way, pushed it off to the side? Unless it had arrived after he'd walked through . . .

Suddenly another kind of panic gripped her. She realized with horror that she'd lost sight of Howard. She had hesitated too long, had allowed the sight of the bird to unhinge her. Its death had been too captivating, too inviting. It had thrown her off balance. Now she had to rush, had to jump over the bird. If he'd only been willing to give in and turn around, then he would have seen that she'd fallen behind.

At one point she fell and tasted dirt, swallowed some and spat out the rest with disgust. The path grew even steeper. He had done this deliberately. He'd killed the bird himself and left it in her path, had known exactly how the sight of it would affect her. A trick, a plan, a plot.

Without any warning the land became flat again, with tall grass and smooth earth. She stood tall, exhausted. Howard, in his wrinkled sweatsuit, was waiting. "Come on, Rebecca," he shouted.

She walked to where he stood, his face aglow. She screamed. In front of her was what she immediately recognized as a freshly dug grave, although she'd never seen one before. She'd been to a cemetery once, but its neat partitioned plots with their carved headstones were nothing like this grave with its rich fresh earth sloppily piled high. A grave perfect in size for a tall man. There was something, not a headstone, but something . . .

She looked at Howard. His face was serious and anguished. He looked much older than sixteen. He nodded at her, silently urging her to step forward.

76

It was a doll. Perched on top of the grave. At first it was difficult to make it out clearly, but slowly it came into focus: it wasn't Heart's Joy or Vitamin Boy as she'd almost expected . . . it was a doll in Evan's likeness.

She shuddered. It was an ivory-colored doll. Someone had taken care to dress it exactly like Evan, in a plaid flannel shirt and neatly pressed tan khaki pants. Even the metal snaps on the flannel shirt were duplicated in miniature form. The khaki pants had a carefully zipped fly and little military buttons on the pockets. The cuffs were perfectly folded. The doll was so lifelike that she almost expected it to speak. Coal-black button-shaped eyes stared back at her—someone had even pasted on eyelashes, possibly made of thread, she guessed. The nose seemed to be an attached beak of wood, as were the ears; even Evan's thick lobes had been mimicked. And that hair . . . that dark wavy hair . . . So natural. Too natural.

Rebecca looked up at the sky. Large black birds, the living relatives of the dead bird she'd just seen, circled above, around the grave, around and around, looking like ferocious black bats. She began to cry. Her nose ran and her throat ached.

"See, Rebecca . . .," Howard said excitedly, "I told you so . . ."

Through her tears she shook her head to silence him. She still held onto the baby doll with its rakishly tilted bonnet. "Take me to Sagana," she sobbed. "Now."

"Why? Are you crazy? Don't you just want to get out of here?"

She took a deep breath and wiped the tears from her eyes with a balled fist. "Howard," she said melodramatically, in a voice remembered from the movies, "I'm going to find her, with or without you!"

He shrugged, looking sixteen again.

Would he rise to the occasion, she wondered. Would he want to be the hero again?

He did. Gallantly, he held out his arm for her. She accepted. Arm in arm they began to walk back the way they'd come, she still wearing the T-shirt, shorts, and sandals in which he'd first met her during her fever; he in the green sweatsuit that now clung to his body like snug saran wrap.

The sun had risen. Rebecca looked back one last time at Evan's grave. The sun had bathed it in a vivid reddish glow, and one of the black birds now sat brazenly on top of it, pushing against the doll with its sharp black beak.

# 12

The walk back downhill seemed quicker. The daylight brought out the shapes of trees and bushes and stones. After a while they emerged from the dense wooded area into a populated clearing. A few huts were scattered about, as though the builders had had momentary inspirations but no coherent plan. Some of the huts looked like they were made of hardened mud. Some were just rocks piled together. Others seemed more sturdily constructed of wood.

She should have been excited, thrilled: Howard was taking her to Sagana. Instead she felt detached. Her mission was now something she had to do, that was all. Had to do. No questions asked. No possibility of turning back, of forgetting the whole thing, of going off somewhere else, of turning to Howard and suggesting a trip to the movies; no possibility of joining up with Rhea; no possibility of leaving the mountain alone, forever, right this second. Just one step in front of another.

She thought about the Sagana she used to know: the little girl with the two plain yellow pigtails; then the woman who'd been her roommate and best friend, who'd listened dotingly to every word of Rebecca's, who'd never seemed interested in anyone else, but who was secretly holding weekly meetings with a group of angry women; then Sagana the pregnant woman with the enormous distorted belly which had reflected Rebecca's own; then Sagana the obsessed mother, diapering and nursing the two small infants; then Sagana the writer of the angry note, Sagana the kidnapper, the megalomaniac, the leader . . . the Amazon Queen.

Howard pointed. "There." Up ahead was a dwelling, not really a hut since it was more elaborate than most. As they neared, she could see that it was composed of a shiny substance, glittering, almost gem-like, nearly transparent. She thought of Eskimo igloos, but this was far more elaborate than any igloo she'd seen in a photograph. Over the large entranceway hung a jet black velvet curtain. The curtain hung like a blanket, without a flutter.

Rebecca knew that this was where she belonged. This was where the journey had been headed all along. This was the culmination. Nothing else mattered. She held out her hand. She was determined to be rid of Howard Geller. "Good-bye, Howard," she said formally. It was imperative that he leave immediately; his presence was now an intrusion.

He didn't take her hand. "Don't you want me to stay?"

"No!" She shook her head. "Definitely not."

Howard grimaced: "I never have any fun." But then he smirked, did a drum riff in the air, and turned and walked away.

Immediately she forgot all about him and boldly, without hesitation, she lifted a corner of the curtain and peered inside. All was darkness. She was not frightened; how could she be when she knew that this was Sagana's home? Rebecca inhaled almost deliriously. This was ecstasy. Sagana had been here, and she would be back again!

But she wanted to see . . . she wanted a glimpse of Sagana's haunt, a hint of her soul's interior. She needed light. There must be a candle somewhere, or a kerosene lamp . . . Sagana would want light at her command, at the touch of her fingers. Rebecca felt in the air with the hand not holding the china doll. Her hand came upon a shelf. Inching her finger along the shelf, she soon found what she wanted—a large wax candle and a box of matches. The candle produced a strong orange flame. She could see.

In the center was a large stately chair of some sort, taller than any chair Rebecca had ever seen. But what was much more astounding, what took her breath away and weakened her knees, were the dolls. Dolls everywhere! Scattered about on the floor, piled haphazardly on top of each other. There was a mass of disembodied heads and arms and legs. They looked like victims of some dreadful calamity, an earthquake, a fire, a tornado.

Too many dolls for her to make out clearly, to distinguish as individuals. She held onto Rhea's nameless baby doll; she didn't want it to dive in and join the others.

Slowly, almost against her will, she allowed some of the dolls to come into focus. They demanded that she get to know them. They no longer looked dead at all, but very much alive though helpless.

Huddled beside one of the legs of the chair was a doll made of feathers, black feathers, with a bird face; its bushy, full stomach made it look pregnant. Next to it was a doll made of brown leather. Leather like the leather strips Howard Geller had been braiding over and over when she'd first awakened from her fever. The leather doll wore leather boots on its leather legs and it had long strips of blonde leather hair . . .

Rebecca was dazzled. So many dolls. She began to fondle them, memorizing them with her eyes and her touch.

Half-hidden, close to the leather doll, was a wooden doll stuck all over with nails and bits of glass. There was

81

also a doll made of straw; a wax doll pierced with needles, which she couldn't bring herself to touch; a young woman doll with cherry-red lips, holding an oriental fan; a doll with two glass eyes and four glass tears frozen eternally on its cheeks; a female clown doll; a black doll with a huge Afro haircut and pointed, nippleless breasts; a doll in an elaborately frilled white wedding dress . . .

A goddess in a tunic on top of a ferocious-looking stag . . . Raggedy Anns and paper dolls with dresses with white tags that fit over their shoulders . . .

A doll in hat, cloak, pointed high-heeled shoes, nylon stockings with black seams on the back, white gloves, a fan, muffler, parasol, handkerchief, handbag . . .

A Shirley Temple doll with masses of ringlets, round blue eyes and pink cheeks, a Snow White doll, an Aunt Jemima doll . . .

A Janus doll which especially intrigued her so that she held onto it for a very long time . . . with two faces, each partially covered by a hood; rapidly, obsessively, she began turning the doll so that over and over the male weeping face turned into the female laughing face and vice versa . . .

An Alice in Wonderland doll . . .

A Betsy Wetsy, which she remembered vividly from her own childhood because it was able to drink from a tiny bottle and then soil its diaper with the water . . .

An Orphan Annie doll with curly red hair and bulging, popping marble eyes . . .

A Cinderella doll and her cruel stepmother and her two evil stepsisters . . .

A Sleeping Beauty with closed eyes and a dreamy smile . . .

A doll wearing dark glasses and holding a pair of crutches . . .

A Tiny Tears whose eyes slowly closed when Rebecca rocked her . . .

A Little Miss Echo containing a tape recorder. "Hello," said Rebecca in a reverent whisper . . . "Hello," whispered back Little Miss Echo, equally reverent, equally dazed . . .

A Thirstee Cry Baby who gurgled in Rebecca's arms . . .

A kissing doll who kissed Rebecca and clung to her face . . . A tall doll, the size of a real child, with a Magic Ring, begging to be pulled . . . Rebecca pulled the ring . . . "Come play with me," said the doll in a whimsical fairy-tale voice. "Come touch me and come tickle me. Caress my round breasts, they are designed to delight. Caress my firm childish yet womanly thighs. I'll tickle you back, I'll touch you too, oh yes, I promise I will!" Rebecca pulled the magic ring a second time and then a third time and then a fourth. Each time the doll recited its erotic plea. "Come play with me," it purred and crooned in its delicious voice, over and over . . .

"Come play with me," repeated Rebecca in the doll's voice, not in her own. "Come play with me!" On her hands and knees, dazed, she crawled over the many dolls in front of her, all around her . . . It seemed to take forever; there were too many dolls, dolls to climb over and under, dolls to toss aside, dolls to wiggle between. She looked at her hands. She was no longer clutching Rhea's baby doll. Somehow it had gotten free. She looked around for it, missing its maddened grin, feeling lost and dizzy inside the maze of smiling, frowning, crying, gurgling, wetting, happy, sad, silent, talking dolls. And yes, she could see Rhea's doll, now seated beside the leather doll, both beside the legs of that tall, stately chair. Rebecca crawled to it.

Perhaps she could draw strength from the pretend-blues. Just like the old days! Gimme a pig foot and a bottle of beer . . . She and Saggie always sang together, on stage, unbeatable, untameable . . .

She picked up the leather doll in one hand and Rhea's baby doll in the other.

*Rub it in rub it out*

(Sang the leather doll)

*Rub it all all about!*

(Sang the baby doll)

*Do it good do it fast*
*Do it like it's gonna last!*

(Sang the baby doll)

*Do it wild do it hot*
*Do it like a lady I'm not!*

(Sang the leather doll)

*Rub it in rub it out*

(Sang both dolls together)

*Rub it in rub it out, Oh Yeah!*

(Sang both dolls together)

The leather doll gently placed her palm upon the other doll's face. *Rub it in.* The baby doll sashayed her hips and purred, a humming, throaty sound—*Oh yessssss I'll be your dear . . .*

84

Rebecca lay back and stretched, kicking dolls aside; the leather doll and the baby doll fell and nestled together on her stomach like two best friends. She lay, watching them rise and then slowly fall each time she exhaled, then rise again . . .

The black velvet curtain parted. Rebecca, on her back, could see two women staring in at her. The two women seemed much larger than life, framed as they were in the entranceway. One dark haired, one a redhead.

The two women drew back simultaneously and the black curtain fell closed. It hung as still as it had before. "Ssh," whispered Rebecca to the leather doll and the baby doll. She was certain that she could hear the two women outside whispering together, scheming together. Were they deciding what to do with the new doll in town?

The velvet curtain parted once more and the two women entered. They were both tall and they stooped slightly. The redhead entered first, the brunette second. Their eyes were calm. Both wore high boots and short white tunics. The brunette's hair was shoulder length and loose, the redhead's past her waist and thick and bushy. Without warning, they sprang forward together as though on cue, like a well-trained trapeze act. Producing a long rope, they began to tie Rebecca up. Neither of them said a word. She scratched and clawed, but they were far too professional to be bothered. The redhead tied a handkerchief around Rebecca's mouth.

Rebecca imagined what she must look like: a woman wrapped in a thick jump rope, the kind of rope that she and Saggie had loved to play with for hours on the grass, ignoring the other children playing Tag and Hopscotch . . . *Fire Fire False Alarm, I fell into my boyfriend's arms, How many kisses did I receive, Ten,*

*Twenty, Thirty!* Saggie had always been better at jumping rope than she'd been; more agile, quicker to hop up and down on time so that her legs were never entangled by the rope . . .

The two silent women seemed satisfied with their work. They both tossed their hair back, then wiped the sweat from their brows, and once again, as though on cue, walked together toward the hut's opening and disappeared through the velvet curtain.

Rebecca closed her eyes and trembled, ashamed of her weakness in front of so many tiny inquisitive faces. She imagined that somewhere in the hut an unsympathetic doll laughed.

# 13

At first she struggled, twisting and turning, but soon she realized that such actions were useless. And then she felt calm. She accepted that she was now in Sagana's hands.

She was exhausted. In spite of the ropes she was able to make a sort of fetal position of her body and was able to relax enough to fall into a deep sleep in which, if she dreamed of anything at all, she dreamed of blackness.

When she awoke she could hear footsteps outside the hut. The velvet curtain was flung open. The two warrior women, her captors, appeared once more. They entered the hut, working again as a synchronized team. Once inside, they stood in front of the curtain, waited a moment, and then each lifted a corner of the curtain.

Something stirred outside; she could see a flash of color, of movement, and then suddenly—too suddenly—there stood Sagana, right there, between the two women, in front of the black curtain. It was Sagana, she was sure. But this was a Sagana transformed into an ideal. This was a Queen. She wore her yellow hair parted in the center and loose, and it looked as though hundreds of golden arrows grew from her scalp. On her body was a transparent colorless long gown. Through the fabric Rebecca could see Sagana's flesh. Rebecca could even see the black bird-shaped birthmark on her hip. The birthmark. Sagana had a bird perched permanently on her hip and the sight of it made Rebecca catch her breath . . . But why? She wanted, she needed to remember something about that birthmark . . .

She was distracted by something shining near Sagana's ear, through her fine yellow hair. It was a silver half-moon earring, the same as worn by Rhea. The half-moon must be their symbol, but of what she wasn't sure . . . Hadn't one of the goddesses, the angry one with all those bows and arrows, been the Goddess of the Moon?

So slowly that at first Rebecca thought she was imagining it, Sagana began to move. The two women followed their Queen as she passed by Rebecca and headed toward the tall chair. Her throne. Sagana sat down. Her shimmering garment flowed around her. The redhead and the brunette stood, silent as ever, on either side of their Queen, with their arms crossed over their chests.

Sagana nodded at them and they came forward. They gently untied Rebecca. They helped her to sit up and then returned to their posts beside Sagana.

Rebecca sat, painfully aware that she and Sagana had exchanged roles. Now she was the ungainly, awkward one, unsure where to place her chafed knees, nervous about hiding her dirty fingernails.

At that moment the black curtain began wildly twisting, and Sagana smiled at last, meeting Rebecca's eyes, as a thunderstorm flooded the world outside. She nodded, and the two women stepped out into the storm.

"Rebecca," Sagana said, still smiling, "Welcome to the mountain. Sorry about the ropes. But I wanted to be sure you'd wait for me."

Rebecca was startled. She had expected Saggie's

voice to be different, but it wasn't. It wasn't a Queen's voice. It was the voice Rebecca had always known. She could speak to this voice. "I came to take Lily back with me," she said, although she was shaking. Rebecca tried to sound firm. "She's my daughter."

Sagana stopped smiling. She sighed. "Are you sure? Becky, can't you see that I did you and Lily a favor? I rescued you from one another."

"She's still my daughter!"

"Face it, you're really not much of a mother. You're really not much of anything, are you?" Sagana laughed, but Rebecca recognized that laugh. It meant that Sagana wasn't really amused.

"Saggie, how can you say that? We used to have such fun together. I was special to you."

"You don't really know what we used to have together. And you certainly don't know what you were to me. How could you? You don't have the slightest idea of who you are."

"Yes I do. I'm still Rebecca. I'm sure of myself. I'm your faithful best friend." She tried to keep sarcasm out of her voice. She didn't want to anger Sagana.

"So you're Faithful Rebecca. Isn't that nice."

"Yes. I have been faithful. No matter what you've become. Saggie," her voice broke, "I don't recognize you."

Sagana spoke gently. "I've just become myself. That's all. Finally. The woman I've always wanted to be." She leaned forward and grasped the arms of her chair. "You do recognize me. You always knew that this woman was there, inside of me. I've just freed her. I've freed her fury."

Rebecca didn't know what Sagana was talking about. But at least they were talking to each other. They

89

weren't enemies. She felt as drawn to Saggie as she had always been. Maybe Saggie would return to New York with her. She took a deep breath. "Saggie, why did you run away from me? Why are you here?"

"Becky, can't you see? We're building a new world. A world of strong women. Women who don't wait on men, who don't live their lives to please and seduce men. Women who love . . . each other."

"But I have looked around here," Rebecca cried. "And I met Rhea. You can't possibly love a woman like Rhea. I know you too well. She could never be a substitute for me!"

Sagana looked thoughtful for a minute. She crossed her legs. "I've had a lot of thinking to do. About why I left that note for you to find. Now that you're here I know why. And so do you."

"I do?"

"Yes. I was inviting you to join us here. I was giving you a chance. And I was right. You followed me here because you want to be one of us. I was right." Sagana stared into Rebecca's eyes.

"No! I'm fine the way I am. We were happy until you ruined everything. If you don't want me the way I am, fine. Just give me Lily and I'll go home. You'll come to me one day, begging my forgiveness!"

Sagana rose from her throne. She looked angry. "You're such a liar. You don't care about Lily. Or me. You really came here to find Evan, didn't you? Your precious Evan. You guessed that he came here, didn't you?"

"So what if I did?" Rebecca stood too.

"You're disgusting, Becky. Disgusting. You care more about a man who never loved you than you do about your own daughter!"

90

"Well, where is he? What's happened to him?" Rebecca wasn't sure she wanted Sagana to answer her. She and Sagana were standing face to face now. Rebecca felt diminished, though, beside Sagana in her flowing dress.

Sagana put her hands on her hips. "You think you loved Evan because there was something special about him. But he was really so ordinary, so bland. He was like cottage cheese. Like most men. You wanted him only because he didn't want you as much as other men wanted you. It was so obvious. He seemed to want me more, didn't he?"

"No! I don't remember that."

"You don't? Oh. I see." Now Sagana looked vaguely amused. "Anyway, Evan knew a little of my plans: a commune, a new world. He saw my ad in the paper and he begged to come. He also said he wanted to get away from you."

"I don't believe you!"

"As for his death . . . Well, everyone dies sooner or later."

Rebecca grimaced. "Whatever you say. But why is Howard Geller here? You didn't know him in New York, did you?"

Sagana stepped back. She looked around the hut, then back at Rebecca. "Little Howard. Well, let's just say that he came here thinking he was going to be Adam. But this time Eve had other plans. We haven't even gotten around to him yet. But we will. We do need daughters, Becky. It's really simple. He's expendable, though."

Rebecca gasped. "Are you going to do to Howard what you did to Evan?"

"I didn't do anything to Evan. Ever." Sagana began to walk around the hut, looking at the dolls. "Rebecca, forget about Evan. Listen to me. This is what you're going to have to do. Tonight you're going to renounce the life you've led in front of all the women here. And then you'll join us. You'll be happy. We'll be happy, I promise." She smiled.

Rebecca noticed that Saggie's eyeglasses were still slightly crooked, just like always. At least that hadn't changed. She closed her eyes. Their friendship had been flawed, not perfect as she'd always felt. She'd been duped. But she didn't have to stand for any of this. She was at last going to present her side of things. The accused was going to defend herself. She would refute the entire case of the prosecution. She drew back her shoulders. "Sagana, I won't renounce my life. I've loved my body. I've been a seductress. I've flirted and teased. I've had every right to do so! And I'm taking Lily home with me."

Sagana shook her head and stared at her coldly. Her voice was icy. "Becky, I feel sorry for you. You haven't even been listening to me."

"Saggie, don't you remember how much fun we had as kids? Remember the games? The pretendblues? Sharkie? And all the games with the dolls . . ."

"You're right. We did have fun playing games with the dolls." Sagana sounded angry, scornful. "So you want to play with dolls now? We can do that. Absolutely. I love playing with dolls." She picked up the doll nearest her. It was the wax doll pierced with needles, a doll that Rebecca hadn't been able to bring herself to touch earlier. Then she bent down and reached for another doll. To Rebecca's surprise, she picked up Rhea's mad baby doll. Holding them aloft, one in each hand, she walked toward Rebecca. Instinctively, Rebecca stepped back.

"I," said Sagana, speaking for Rhea's doll which she

held close to Rebecca's face, "have sinned, have plotted against a woman who had nothing but my happiness at heart. I need to repent, I must repent!" Here Sagana laughed quickly. "But how can I repent when my body is so impervious to pain?"

"Have no fear," shouted the wax doll, "for I bear enough needles for two. Trust me. Become me. You'll feel more pain than you'll be able to stand."

"Yes," cried Rhea's doll, which Rebecca now understood was being used to represent Rhea herself. "I am you!"

Sagana removed the needle piercing the spot where the wax doll's heart would be. She held it in the air and then savagely thrust it back into the same spot. The wax doll was silent, but the Rhea doll screamed.

Sagana laughed again. She put the two dolls down and then grabbed the Janus doll. At once its sad male face began to speak in a recognizable voice that sent shivers through Rebecca. "I need you; I followed you, didn't I? I followed you here because I love, need, want you." There was a silence during which Sagana continued to hold the male face high. Suddenly, "My God!" Evan's voice said, in a bewildered, almost boyish tone, "I've been . . ." and Sagana turned the Janus doll around so that the eager, smiling female face greeted Rebecca now. It remained silent, but its great smile told all.

Sagana let the doll tumble to the ground. She picked up the Tiny Tears. She made her voice lisping and small. "Oh, I'm just a baby. Just an unloved, unwanted baby. My mother doesn't love me. Oh oh oh . . . I'll have to go away with the one who will raise me to be a real woman . . ." Sagana rocked the doll in her arms so that its eyelids dropped shut. Gently Sagana placed Tiny Tears down.

"Stop it," cried Rebecca. Her skin crawled as she watched Sagana pick up another doll, the tall doll the size of a real child. She held it in her arms, swaying with it, and they looked like oddly mismatched dance partners. Rebecca wanted to reach out and prevent Sagana from pulling the doll's Magic Ring, but it was too late; already that beautiful voice was delivering its seductive plea: "Come play with me. Come touch me and tickle me. Caress my round breasts . . ."

Sagana spoke now in her own voice. "Rebecca," she asked, "don't you recognize yourself? All you want is to be caressed, touched, licked, by men! But there's more to life than that. Watch how easily that needy side of you can be destroyed. Watch." She brutally twisted the right arm of the doll until it came loose of its socket and fell with a timid noise to the floor. "Watch, Rebecca, watch," and she twisted the other arm even more violently so that it came out in an easy rush. Sagana pulled the Magic Ring again. "Come play with me," the doll began. "Listen!" commanded Sagana. "Listen to how desperate and pathetic you sound. Help me, Rebecca, help me to destroy that sound. Come twist the leg—like this—come . . ." She began twisting the doll's left leg from side to side so that the doll appeared momentarily exotic and tantalizing. Rebecca wanted to join in. It was tempting, very tempting, to destroy this doll. She was starting to hate this doll who was once again reciting, "Caress my firm, childish yet woman-like thighs. I'll tickle you back." Sagana had removed the left leg; she now held onto the doll's right leg. "This one is yours, Rebecca," she nearly sang.

94

Rebecca took a small step forward. She raised her arm. She was ready to rip the doll's pink leg from its socket. Sagana smiled. "And after that, we'll rip out its hair, strand by strand, and then we'll pluck out your eyes . . . By the time we're through with her, with you, there'll be nothing left. You can be born anew."

Rebecca moved forward slowly, dreamily; she imagined the doll as it would soon be, sightless, hairless, limbless . . .

The doll's leg felt slippery in her grasp. Sagana placed her hand on Rebecca's shoulder. Rebecca succumbed, pulled sharply. The leg fell just as it was supposed to, but then in the very next instant, almost without time to complete a breath, she rebelled and pushed Sagana's hand off her shoulder. She reached down and scooped up the two legs and the two arms in her own arms. Cradling them and panting heavily she squared off to face Sagana, who lifted the disfigured naked doll up high and pulled its Magic Ring one last time. Just as it began its final plea she threw it against the wall of the hut. The doll bounced off, losing one plastic blue eye in the process, and then landed, dazed, in an upright position right beside the leather doll.

Rebecca had no idea why she cradled the useless limbs, nor what she was about to say as she began to speak, angrily and breathlessly: "It's not going to be that simple for you, Sagana. I'm part of you—as I am. Not as you want me to be."

The velvet curtain parted and the two women came inside. They wore capes that were dripping wet from the storm. Sagana spoke softly, although Rebecca sensed that she was still furious. "You haven't been listening to me. You haven't faced the truth about yourself yet. I'm going to have to leave you now. I think you need to be alone again."

The two women approached Rebecca. This time she knew better than to struggle as they tied her up. Before they left her in the hut, Sagana blew out the candle.

Rebecca was abandoned, imprisoned within a world of dolls, feeling like one herself.

# 14

Perhaps she slept. Perhaps not. It was so dark inside the hut. She wished she could see the dolls all around her.

"I felt guilty."

She gasped. Someone was talking to her. One of the dolls? Had one of the dolls come to life? Which one?

She heard a match being struck once, twice. Her body tightened.

On his third try, Howard Geller lit the candle. He came and stood above her. She felt an odd comforting sense of familiarity. He hesitated a moment and then untied her. He still wore the soiled green sweatsuit.

He looked at her accusingly. "I felt guilty. Guilty! So I came back to see if you were okay." He sighed. "I'm still not having any fun."

Rebecca barely heard him. "My best friend is . . ." she shook her head in disbelief, "an . . . Amazon. Sagana's so different. I just can't believe it's her. I'm going to have to live alone." She realized that she was about to break down and cry in front of him, but she stopped herself. Had she come so far just to confide in a confused sixteen-year-old boy? She grew angry with him. Who did he think he was in her life? What role did he think he'd been cast to play?

"I'm still not sure, really," Howard said, helping her up, "which one of you two I should be helping out. Maybe I'd have more fun with Sagana and the others."

"No," said Rebecca, suddenly concerned for him. "I don't think so. Sagana isn't going to be your Eve."

"I guess for now it's got to be you because I'm not frightened of you." He looked around. "These dolls are creepy. Let's get off this mountain and go home."

"No. I'm not going."

"Not going? What's going on?"

"I can't go with you yet because I've got to find Lily. Don't think I'm not grateful to you. I'm well aware that I probably won't be able to find my way down this mountain without your help. You're probably my only chance. And if you don't want to help me find Lily, there's nothing I can do. You're your own man, you make your own decisions. You've insisted on making that clear to me all along."

"This is nuts," he muttered.

"Do you think I like this role? Me being brave and maternal? Do I really know what I'm doing? But what choice do I have?"

He started to bob his head up and down while doing one of his drum riffs in the air.

Quickly, she decided to change her tactic. "Just please," she lowered her eyes, "please, take me to Lily. I'm sure you know where she is. Please help me." She placed her hand to her throat and tried to look faint.

As always, Howard couldn't resist melodrama; she'd counted on this. She sensed that all he wanted, deep down, was to get a chance to act like the hero. He chose for now a squinty-eyed pose. He grunted something which sounded like yes. So he would play the strong silent type, Rebecca guessed. That was fine with her.

Together, they peered both ways before venturing out into the darkness. She held tightly onto his arm.

# 15

Nights on the mountain were blacker than city nights. In New York there were neon signs and street lamps and billboards splashy with rainbow day-glo colors, but on the mountain the darkness was complete. If they had a flashlight, anything . . . But bravely they walked forward, Rebecca wishing she could trust Howard completely.

They didn't speak to each other. She thought about Lily: it wasn't too late to truly be her mother, was it? Though before she had refused to mother her at all. Lily remained a mystery to her. She couldn't imagine her daughter very well. Even now as she searched for her, she couldn't quite fathom the existence of her own child. Yet more than anything in the world she wanted to hold Lily in her arms.

When she first brought Lily home from the hospital, she hadn't known what to do with her. Lily seemed too fragile, and Rebecca sometimes imagined herself digging her sculptured painted fingernails deep into the baby's skull. Then she would panic and think that Sagana had read her mind. While the baby lay crying and screaming in her crib, she wouldn't be able to go to her, to pick her up in her arms, to offer comfort. Sagana would come instead and feed Lily and change her and rock her and help her to fall asleep, and then she would refuse to speak to Rebecca.

Sagana's baby was a quiet, restful baby, not like Lily who jumped and screamed at the slightest noise and who was never, never satisfied. Lily would start to suck at the bottle Rebecca forced herself to hold, but quickly she'd fall asleep, refusing to take any more milk. Then Rebecca would carry her back to the crib, her hands shaking, and she would start to tiptoe out of the room—but at precisely that moment the baby would wake up crying again, hungry. And Sagana would call angrily from the other room, "She's hungry, why don't you ever feed her?" And Rebecca would say, "I tried!" and then she'd try one more time but it would happen again, exactly the same way. Lily would fall right to sleep after sucking at the bottle only an instant. And then she'd wake up hungry moments later, back in her crib. And Rebecca would run out of the apartment, leaving Sagana with both babies. Sagana's Diana was a plucky, healthy infant, but Lily came down with coughs and earaches and fevers. And when she walked the streets with Lily, nobody looked at her as they used to. She never felt those same approving, sensual glances of men, the glances she expected and needed. And there was never enough sleep. And the worst nights were Wednesday nights, when Sagana left with Diana, and she was alone with Lily.

Really, she had known her daughter for such a short time before Sagana ran off with her. They were virtually strangers.

Sagana had seemed healthier and happier than ever when the babies were born: she was fresh and energetic, shuttling between babies. Exhausted, Rebecca applied lotions and gels and creams to her own skin, afraid that the wear and misery would etch itself out in telltale lines on her face and neck and hands. She would rub creams over her hips and breasts until her body became slippery. She felt sorry for herself. She wanted a good night's sleep. She wanted to feel the freedom to bring a man home any time, night or day. Instead there would be only occasional jittery sleeps of short duration. And then the baby would cry and wake her.

Sometimes Rebecca would tiptoe in to stare down at her sleeping baby in order to convince herself yet one more time that all this was real, that this had happened, and that there was another human life, now and forever, that would demand the world of her. Somehow Evan had made her pregnant; she refused to think about when.

Lily preferred sleeping on her stomach. Rebecca smiled, suddenly pleased that she remembered that fact. It was something intimate about her daughter. Diana slept mostly on her back. But Lily slept on her stomach with her head always facing the left. Yes, Rebecca felt much closer to her, remembering that.

Howard broke the silence. "We're almost at the hut where I think Lily sleeps."

"Won't someone be there with her?"

"I don't know. They have funny ideas about bringing up kids." He paused. "I wish my parents had left me alone more often."

Soon they came upon a small brown hut. This hut had none of the splendor and elegance of the hut in which Sagana kept her many dolls. What if Lily wasn't alone, she wondered. What if Sagana herself was there or her warriors or Rhea . . . And of course someone would be sitting with the baby, because nobody would leave a baby alone.

She wondered whether Lily would remember her. If Lily had been almost a stranger to her when they'd lived together, she'd be a total stranger to her now. She'd heard that babies changed so rapidly that every week they seemed to be new people. Perhaps Lily had changed so much that she'd melted into the mountain, perhaps she no longer existed.

"Howard, really, what do we do if someone is in there with her?"

He widened his eyes. "I don't know." His movie-hero voice had completely vanished.

A scratchy-looking strip of burlap served as the curtain over the entrance. Was Lily considered a second-class citizen because of her mother? Or was Diana being treated the same way? Did it have something to do with Amazons refusing to dote upon their children in the same fashion that ordinary American mothers did? Although the Sagana she remembered back home had doted upon both Diana and Lily as much as any TV mom . . .

There was no way to peer in undetected to see whether Lily slept quietly alone; the burlap was too thick. Rebecca doubted once again that Lily was even inside, for her Lily . . . the Lily she knew . . . cried and screamed and tossed and turned in her sleep. The slightest noise bothered her Lily. Surely even their stealthy approach would have disturbed her baby.

What were they to do now? Howard was silent. Rebecca moved her gaze from the burlap to Howard; he looked away. She had the feeling that any second he might bolt. At that, without another second's hesitation, she lifted the burlap curtain.

A tall candle stood on a low wooden table giving off enough light so that Rebecca was able to see the makeshift wooden crib that held a sleeping child. So Howard had been trustworthy after all; he'd led her first to Evan's grave, then to Sagana, and at last to Lily.

He didn't follow her inside.

The baby lay sleeping on her back beneath a plaid

cotton blanket. Rebecca felt betrayed. Was this Lily? Lily always slept on her belly with her head turned to the left. This baby stirred a bit in its sleep, but didn't wake. She had blonde hair now, growing in silky waves. Her nose was tiny and her skin pale. She breathed in and out deeply, her pink lips parted a fraction. One of her delicate hands fluttered in its sleep and then clutched at a corner of the plaid blanket.

Yes, this was Lily. Rebecca was sure. It wasn't exactly love that she felt as she gazed down at her sleeping child, but it was definitely something strong. Although she knew that she needed to lift Lily gently from the crib without waking her, she wasn't ready to reach down and claim her daughter. By what right did she make such a claim, after all? Lily would awaken, terrified by this strange woman, and she would wail and scream and attract the attention of the women—her new mothers. And perhaps they were more like mothers to her than she herself could ever be.

Lily slept peacefully, her shining lips coming together for an instant then parting again, her tissue-thin eyelids fluttering. Rebecca's hands remained at her sides. She couldn't move. She sensed Howard's presence beside her.

"Let's go," he said. "Come on, Rebecca."

"I can't. I can't pick her up."

Howard shook his head. He spoke in a whisper. "Well, don't look at me."

"I can't do it. I can't."

Howard sighed, looking older than sixteen once again, and reached down and lifted Lily. Lily didn't even make a sound.

# 16

They stood poised outside, ready to begin their flight from the mountain. Rebecca felt precariously balanced, but Howard, holding Lily in his arms, seemed composed. "Be quiet," he said. "We'll walk down the mountain. There's a lake. There'll be some boats. They're easy to row. I can do that. We'll get into one of the boats and soon we'll be away from here. On the other side of the shore there's a small town with a bus station. I still have some money. We can take a bus home to New York."

"I don't even remember how I got here," Rebecca said. "The first thing I remember, actually, is . . . you. Braiding leather. I don't remember a bus or a town or water or boats."

"Just follow me." He started walking.

Rebecca knew that she should take Lily in her own arms, but she couldn't. Not yet. Surely she would drop the baby and she would break. Or she would awaken and scream. No. Howard seemed to be handling her so well. He could hold her for a while more. Besides, what they were embarking upon was dangerous. Very dangerous. Rebecca wanted to believe Howard's story of water and a boat and easy access to busses traveling back and forth to New York City, but it sounded unbelievable on the mountain.

She grew used to seeing in the dark and became more confident with each step. Things didn't seem as threatening as before. She would be ready to take Lily in her arms soon.

But then gradually there were noises in the distance. Faint and vague. She said nothing to Howard, hoping that she was imagining them. But they continued. "Maybe we should go some other way."

"This is the only path that leads to the water," he whispered. "We have to follow it."

"Maybe it's only the wind," Rebecca whispered back, knowing as she said it that it was no wind. She was even beginning to think she could hear chanting of some sort. A rushing exotic rhythmic sound.

Howard stopped short and blocked Rebecca from going any further. "Behind the trees," he nervously whispered, and began pushing her, with Lily still asleep in his arms, toward the shelter of a few broad trees off the side of the path.

In the darkness she was able to make out the source of the noise and the rhythm: the women. Heading toward them, not on the path but weaving through the trees, came a group of the Amazons. Each of the women was holding something in her arms; Rebecca feared inexplicably that each held a dead animal, the dead carcass of a goat or sheep or even a dog or cat. Perhaps the women were about to perform a sacrifice to a goddess, or perhaps a sacrifice just for the sake of the kill itself . . . But it was dolls the women carried, not dead animals but lifeless dolls! Each woman carried a doll in her arms, a miniature of a human form.

The moon rose suddenly and vividly, a full, round moon, illuminating the women so that they looked like ghosts as they approached in long swishing white dresses.

Surely she and Howard would be spotted as they passed by. There was nowhere else to hide, though, and so they stood, pressed stomach to stomach to flatten themselves out. Lily still rested, now held tightly against Howard's chest. Above the child they stared silently into each other's eyes.

The women continued their march toward them, and Rebecca realized that the chant was really a low humming sound, a long nonsense syllable with no beginning or end, unchanging in tone or pitch. A physical extension of their slender throats. It hinted of bonds and secrets that she would never understand. Was it a sound of power, of violence?

She held her breath and she could see Howard doing the same, as they both waited for the humming Amazons in white to pass by. But Sagana and her women had other ideas: they paused in a clearing almost parallel to where Rebecca and Howard stood. Then, as a single body, they gathered together to form a perfect circle. Only the narrow path separated them.

Still in the circle, the women seated themselves. There were about twenty women. They looked aroused. They looked beautiful. And there sat Sagana, dressed like all the others in white, but still standing out, her face lit with desire. She was the most beautiful. On either side of Sagana sat the two warrior women, the redhead and the brunette. Beside the redhead sat the first woman Rebecca had encountered on the mountain, the small ephemeral creature with the blazing eyes and booming voice. Rebecca suspected that this was Mara, who'd wanted to rid the mountain of her through drastic means. Next to Mara was a black woman who looked slightly older than the others. Her graying hair was cropped short in tight individual curls. Before Rebecca could look at all the others, a movement on one side of the circle caught her eye. Someone was fidgety, impatient. It was Rhea, who looked angry and not aroused at all.

Just then, Sagana spoke. One word: "Now." Her voice was throaty and sensual. Every woman in the circle, except Sagana, raised her doll up high. Rebecca recognized the dolls from Sagana's hut. A woman wearing aviator-shaped eyeglasses and a layered haircut held the doll with the dark glasses and crutches, and a broad-shouldered blonde with braids held the doll in the elaborately frilled wedding dress. The delicate-looking Mara held her doll lower than the other women and Rebecca couldn't see it clearly at first. As though Mara knew that Rebecca was watching, she raised her arm suddenly and lifted her doll even higher than all the others. In her hands was a doll version of Howard Geller with a wide open silently screaming mouth.

This doll was definitely Howard, with his bare chest and baggy faded blue jean overalls. Something sparkled brightly on the fabric of the overalls and Rebecca was sure that even the tiny mirrors sewn into the coarse dungaree material had been duplicated. His shaggy mop of hair had also been perfectly recreated. What was most awful, though, were its bare feet: there was something hideous about the feet of this doll, its tiny realistically rendered toes. Rhea now raised her doll higher than Mara's. Rebecca wasn't surprised to see Rhea's mad baby doll again. Sagana still sat holding her doll on her lap with her arms on top of it, blocking it from view.

The other women continued to hold their dolls high. Rebecca sensed that they were waiting for Sagana to lift hers as a signal that the proceedings—whatever they were—could begin. Rebecca trembled—what kind of secret ritual would they perform? And why did it feel so exciting to watch them? Just at that moment, Sagana began caressing and stroking the hidden doll in her lap. The other women began their humming sound again, that low humming sound in their throats; they watched as Sagana stroked her doll. Rebecca looked at Howard. He stood still, expressionless. Lily slept peacefully in his arms. But her own body was already beginning to feel heated, her heart was already pulsing the familiar erratic rhythms of desire.

Sagana smiled widely and stopped stroking the doll. Slowly, she began lifting it up. Rebecca realized which doll was being unveiled so teasingly: it was the only doll for Sagana, the inevitable choice. What else but the damaged Rebecca-doll, now limbless and missing one eye? The doll that had been murdered back in the hut.

And then the women stopped their throaty purring. Each woman lowered her doll. And then it looked to Rebecca like the dolls were slithering together on their bellies into the center of the circle. Naturally, the women, still holding them, slithered too. The first doll to right itself was the wax doll. Next was the bridal doll in her wedding dress. Then one by one all the dolls stood up, except for the Howard-doll and the Rebecca-doll, who were placed on their backs. The other dolls gathered around the two prone forms. Then, like birds of prey descending, all the dolls swooped down at once upon the two prone dolls. Rebecca saw Rhea, still holding her baby doll, hang back from the other women and then slip away. None of them seemed to notice. They were too involved with their erotic game. If Rebecca joined in, she and Sagana would be reunited. They would be best friends again. And it was as though she could feel them all so deeply inside her body, could feel their hands and legs and beaks and mouths all over . . . and she could feel them inside and on top of Howard too. Again and again. She began to strain forward, to move toward the circle and spread herself out, a beautiful living doll . . . She was taking a step, then another, then another, away from the concealment of the tree . . .

Something was thrust into her arms, and from her reverie she realized it was a baby, and then she understood that it was her own baby. Howard, without warning, had given Lily to her. And at that moment, Lily woke up in Rebecca's arms and screamed.

The dolls in the circle scattered, and the women stood up. They looked with one face in the direction of Lily's frightened wails and howls. Sagana threw the Rebecca-doll to the ground and stepped down deliberately on it. She planted her foot on the doll's face. And then she spoke that one word again. "Now," and all the women surged forward, like runners at the start of a race.

Howard grabbed the screaming Lily back from Rebecca, gave her a push, and began to run swiftly along the path. But Rebecca was no runner! And these barefoot women were trained. Howard had said they ran every day . . .

But what choice did she have? She began to run in her T-shirt and shorts and sandals. It seemed like ages since Lily had first screamed, but surely it was only an instant, less than an instant. And she was actually keeping pace with Howard! Racing forward, they moved to a crazed, frantic beat, hoping against hope to outrun the women warriors pursuing them.

# 17

The sun was beginning to rise, but the moon remained in the sky as well. Large black birds followed the runners with a parallel flight of their own. Rebecca ran, expertly avoiding fallen branches as though she'd known this path and its obstacles all her life. Howard raced beside her. Lily continued to cry and pulled at Howard's long hair with tiny desperate fists.

Rebecca turned around. She couldn't resist glancing at the women running close together behind her, running swiftly, almost demonically. Sagana led them all, her blonde hair streaming behind her. Mara ran only a little behind Sagana, with her mouth open, her arms held high, and her hands clenched into furious fists, not like any runner Rebecca had ever seen. None of the women resembled any of the runners she'd ever seen before. These women were flying over land.

She turned forward, reawakened into panic, wondering how it was possible that she and Howard were eluding them, were running more quickly! The weather on the mountain had always been so uncanny, so unpredictable, not governed by any natural laws, and now her running was the same, defying the facts. What was allowing her to be the fastest, the best runner of all?

Ahead of them like a mirage appeared the body of water that Howard had earlier promised. Even if they made it as far as the water, certainly there the women would seize the opportunity to descend upon them, to pull them apart limb by limb as Sagana had done to the Rebecca-doll. No matter; she had to keep running, one foot flying in front of the other, had to run though her heart was going to explode. The water was their only hope. She had to escape. To escape from . . . No, this was not the time to question, this was the time to run, because if she started questioning herself now, surely she would trip, she would fall over the rocks and branches in her way, she would lose her footing . . .

But she couldn't stop one recurrent thought: Lily's safety. What if Howard fell or was captured? What if Lily was hurt? If the women took Lily back, would she be punished for the sins of her mother? What if they did somehow escape, did really pull this off . . . What could she offer Lily?

They were getting near the water now. The path no longer seemed endless. She refused to turn around again to see how close behind her they were. No time to look back, no matter that she imagined the warmth of their breath on her neck. The water was there, offering a way out. Yes, there were boats in the water! Only a few, and even from a distance they looked old and flimsy, but at least they were there.

Howard was beside her, breathing loudly, trying to keep up. She was so fast now that he had to strain. She began to smell something. Or perhaps she hadn't really smelled it yet, perhaps she only imagined it. Without hesitation she turned around to face the women once again. Behind them she saw the flames. Rebecca stopped short.

Up on the mountain, from where they had come, the world was on fire. Sagana turned around. Mara followed suit. Then, one by one, all the women turned around. They stood in a huddled group, breathing loudly, catching their breath. The flames were growing higher. Rebecca heard Sagana's anguished cry of "Diana!" and then she saw Sagana run. She ran up the path now, retracing her steps, a difficult climb—she tripped and fell to her knees and righted herself; there was no grace now in her movements, only panic. All the women joined her, equally clumsy, equally desperate. They were all attempting to run toward the fire, to rescue what they could, perhaps hoping to surround it and smother it by the very power and force of their presence.

Rebecca was frozen in flight only a few feet from the boats, hardly able to understand, let alone rejoice in the fact that she had been set free. She took a few steps in the direction of the women, thinking that she had to go with them, that she deserved to die, because surely it was the candle she'd left burning in Lily's hut that had tipped over . . .

Just then she saw—or thought she saw, since at first she couldn't believe her eyes—Rhea running in a different direction. She was not with the other women. She was running away from them, disappearing into a group of trees. Where was she going? Perhaps she knew a shortcut to the top of the mountain! But Rebecca knew better, and the knowledge sickened her; she knew that it had been Rhea who had deliberately started the monstrous fire to show her strength, to enact her rebellion. Rhea was running away. Perhaps the voices inside Rhea's head had instructed her in the proper techniques to set the world afire, to be certain that the flames would spread quickly.

Rebecca and Howard watched until Rhea was out of sight. Howard gently placed Lily in Rebecca's arms so that he could begin maneuvering a boat stuck in the mud. Rebecca couldn't take her eyes off the glowing fire and the group of women, made much smaller by the distance. She felt only sorrow now, a sort of tender ache. She felt all alone. And what of Sagana's Diana? Rebecca stared down at Lily, who stared back at her with blue eyes that seemed frozen and enormous. Frightened, she pulled her gaze from the baby and stared again at the women in flight.

Howard called her name, and she understood without turning around to look at him that the boat was ready. He would row them to safety. She waited, unwilling to move, unwilling to take her eyes away from the women, fearing that if she once turned away they would cease to exist. She feared murdering them. But she finally turned around and stepped with the baby in her arms through the mud into the water. The water was cold and stung her bare ankles and calves. The boat was rickety. She seated herself across from Howard, who'd already taken up the oars.

Lily fell asleep, soothed by the sway of the gentle water beneath them. The water seemed never-ending despite the fact that she could already vaguely make out the opposite shore. She and Howard said nothing. She wondered if he was making plans to return to school, or whether, like her, he was just numb. The last time she'd been in the water Rhea had watched her. Now, were she to enter the cool, dark water, she would only hope to drown. Was it possible that they would row to land, leave the boat and walk to a normal town with a bus station? She could no longer see the women. The flames were a faded orange blur. Finally, she felt the horror of the loss of Sagana, Sagana who had always believed that the whole wide world was her cauldron and that she was powerful enough to concoct within it any brew that she pleased. She would miss her so much.

Howard interrupted her. His face was tired, his long

hair matted together. "Rebecca, Sagana's not going to die, you know. She won't give in this easily."

She knew immediately that he was right. And then she closed her eyes and slept, too, her last waking sensation being a vague pleasure for Howard, who was, at last, a hero.

# 18

Lily was asleep in her crib, her fists clenched, just a few feet from where Rebecca lay in her own bed. Rebecca didn't need to peek into the crib to know how Lily looked asleep, her skin rosy and flushed, her eyelids thin and vulnerable. Since their return, she'd been committing Lily, at last, to her memory, to her heart. This time she was determined to be a perfect mother; she could not expect any more chances after this one. She had shut the door to Sagana's room. She didn't want Lily to see any reminders of Sagana.

In the early days back home—she'd only been back from the mountain a month—Rebecca often saw Sagana glaring out at her from Lily's features. Sometimes she saw Evan's mocking face, as well. But never any trace of herself. At such moments she regarded her daughter as suspiciously as Lily regarded her. "A mutual distrust society we've got here, huh?" she asked Lily one day. Lily bared her pearly baby teeth.

Once, during their first week home, Lily kicked out at her, screaming with rage, her face the color of a sunset. Rebecca, losing control, had cried, "You Amazon brat, you!" Lily stopped crying and a hard look crossed her features.

Sometimes Lily seemed cool and detached, not involved enough with her mother to hate her. Then suddenly she'd begin to coo and smile and hold out her arms. At such moments it was Evan Rebecca saw in Lily: the deceitful liar who'd never loved her. Evan had certainly gotten his, though, hadn't he? "Please," Rebecca would whisper to Lily, "please don't become like him." She was unable to bring herself to say "like your father." "Did Sagana murder him, Lily?" she asked, but Lily wasn't speaking yet. Anyway, Rebecca believed that she already knew the answer to that question. She didn't believe that Sagana had murdered Evan. She didn't believe that Sagana could ever murder anyone. Rebecca was certain that such murders were merely Saggie's precious fantasies.

Once, when they were kids, they had played a game of murder with the dolls. It was Saggie's idea: "Let's have Lola Lips kill Aunt Moonlight!" Aunt Moonlight was the kind Hawaiian doll in a grass skirt. She ministered to the ill and needy, she loved animals and children. Lola Lips was her alter ego: "I'm Lola Lips," Saggie would announce, holding the doll in front of her, wiggling its hips in the plastic grass skirt. "I bite and suck. I draw blood." Then she would cackle, that terrible cackle which she'd perfected. "I'm a witch!"

"How can Lola Lips kill Aunt Moonlight if they're part of each other?" Rebecca asked.

"Easy. It's suicide, only it isn't. But," Sagana added thoughtfully, "we have to have a reason . . ."

They sat silently for a few moments. Rebecca wasn't even certain that she wanted Aunt Moonlight dead. Anyway, Lola Lips was much more Saggie's creation than hers. Her own favorite doll was definitely Bitchette, who was large-breasted and had heart shaped lips and curly hair. Bitchette was a seductress and a tease, but she was sensitive and vulnerable too.

"I've got it!" Sagana declared. "Here it is. Aunt Moonlight falls in love with some guy. We'll figure out which doll later. She gets to be a real drip, a real drag . . . She becomes a terrible burden on Lola. All

Aunt Moonlight thinks about is this guy. She talks about nothing else. He's the whole world to her. Lola's going crazy. She wants to be free of this crap! Who can blame her? If she doesn't, she'll die herself. She has no choice."

"Kill or be killed," said Rebecca, feeling swept up by the game. "But we've got to figure out who she loves."

They chose Vitamin Boy because he was the most confident. He was the doll who expected all the women dolls to adore him. In a flash, Vitamin Boy and Aunt Moonlight had center stage. Aunt Moonlight cuddled and cooed beside Vitamin Boy. "I love you, Vitamin Boy," Rebecca crooned as Moonlight. "I love, love, love you . . . I love you, Vitamin Boy. Let's get married and I'll be so good to you . . ."

"Yeah, yeah," answered Saggie as Vitamin Boy in a gruff irritated voice. "Yeah, yeah, whatever you say. Just make sure you fetch my slippers and pipe, don't burn the toast and remember my mistress's birthday . . ."

"Damn!" cried Lola Lips, emerging at last, wild with rage. "No more! Damn you, Vitamin Boy! And even more, damn you, Moonlight! Damn you!"

"Urggh . . . Aargh . . ." Rebecca grasped her own throat and reeled backwards.

The game was over. Saggie was victorious and happy.

"Does this mean," Rebecca asked, "that we can't ever play with Moonlight again? That she's permanently dead?"

Sagana thought for a moment. "No. I guess it's okay to play with her again." She paused, then smiled. "Maybe tomorrow, we'll kill Vitamin Boy."

Vitamin Boy. Evan. Two deaths. They were becoming entangled in her mind. Rebecca remembered her first meeting with Evan. It had been at a party. She arrived at the crowded party feeling especially charming, certain that something exciting was going to happen. She wore a soft black velvet dress and a red rose in her hair. She was standing at the buffet table wondering whether to have some guacamole—but avocadoes were so fattening. A dark-haired man in a herringbone jacket and grey slacks deliberately approached her. This was no surprise. If it hadn't been him, it would have been someone else. It always was.

But he seemed more interested in the dips and crackers and cheeses than in her. Although he asked what her name was and where she lived, he seemed bored by her. He even yawned. She touched the rose in her hair; if it were gone, that might explain his lack of interest. The rose became her talisman, her lucky charm. It was still there. When he wandered away he didn't even look back at her.

She just kept standing there, unable to eat a bite of the guacamole. Never before had something like this happened—to other women perhaps, but never to her.

When he finally returned to the buffet table, she was obsessed with him. Other men had approached her, but she brushed them off. He offered no apology. He acted as though he knew that she'd be waiting for him. He was the only man in the room for her—the only man in the world. She'd never before wanted any one man so much.

She didn't want to lose him. Breathlessly, she asked him to come home with her. He said yes, but throughout the taxi ride home he was silent. She told herself that he was simply playing hard to get. But that was supposed to be the feminine role—her role—and she felt unsettled all over again.

Sagana was sitting on the sofa, barefoot and wearing old grey sweat pants and a sweat shirt, not reading, not watching television. Rebecca was sure that she'd been waiting up for her, although Saggie never would admit it. When she introduced Evan to Sagana, she felt like a blushing teenager. Sagana merely nodded at Evan, watching Rebecca instead.

"Your rose, you know," she pointed, "is askew." At that instant, the rose toppled from Rebecca's hair onto the living room floor. Rebecca expected Evan to bend down and pick it up, but he didn't move. Finally Rebecca bent down and carefully retrieved it. Then, as if to show what she thought of its magical powers now, she offered it to Sagana. "Here, put it in your hair!" She stuck it into Saggie's yellow hair. In her ragged sweat clothes Sagana looked absurd, and Rebecca felt vindicated.

"That looks attractive," Evan said smoothly, and Rebecca wondered why he was more flattering to Sagana than he'd been to her. Kinder to the underdog? Well, he had little at stake with Sagana—she was nothing to him but the roommate of the woman he wanted, the woman by whom he'd been beguiled. He was definitely playing hard to get.

Sagana, laughing, removed the rose from her hair and flung it away. It landed at Rebecca's feet. This time, Evan bent down and picked it up. He held it gingerly, cupped between his hands. For a moment he did nothing with it. Rebecca wondered if he was going to put it in his own thick dark hair. She held her breath. He gently placed the rose on the arm of the sofa, beside Sagana.

Rebecca was sure that, like all of the other men she'd brought home, he'd just want to get her alone in her bedroom. Usually men just made a pretense of talking with Sagana. But not Evan. He seated himself in the armchair across from Sagana. "And what do you do?" he asked Sagana, leaning forward.

"The same as she does," Sagana replied, looking amused, pointing at Rebecca.

"I'm tired," Rebecca announced, even though she wasn't. The truth was that she wanted Evan in her bedroom. She couldn't wait any more. She backed toward the bedroom, still facing Evan and Sagana, neither of whom moved. She was afraid for some reason to turn her back to them. Wasn't he going to join her? But of course he would follow her. Why else had he come home with her?

At last Evan rose. So slowly that Rebecca wouldn't have been surprised to hear his body creak. But no . . . Evan was too graceful, too smooth for that. Standing, he checked the perfect crease of his trousers.

Rebecca arrived at her bedroom. She had no choice but to turn her back to the duo and open the door. Much to her surprise, she heard the sound of Sagana's laughter behind her back. Laughing? At what? Laughter at the sight of Rebecca trapped and on fire, unable to move? Had Evan softly whispered something or made a flippant gesture?

Nobody was going to laugh at her! Nobody. Never. She stepped inside the room and wheeled about violently, breathing hard. Evan was right behind her, almost on top of her. Without a pause, she abruptly thrust her arm past him and shut the door. And then she shuddered. For a long moment they stood facing one another. He seemed disinclined to move closer to her, to touch her as she wanted to be touched, to stroke her, to grab her, to hug her so tightly she would be in almost too much pain—but not quite too much—to bear. Rebecca knew that if she were to slip her own hand beneath her black velvet dress and inside her pink lace panties, she would find that her own flesh was soft and smooth like the dress, and intricately formed and delicate, like the lace. And wet. So wet. Mentally, she tasted herself: a hot, sour liquid, pungent as Chinese mustard and sweet as honey. She was ripe, perfect. Rebecca was beside herself. "Don't you want me?" she begged, incredulous. Her hands mimed a gesture in the air that vaguely resembled a woman disrobing.

"Of course," he answered politely and then turned around as though she weren't there. He seemed to be staring at the closed door behind him.

She began to undress, wondering whether this was a mistake, wondering whether she ought to be undressing him first, slowly unbuttoning the small white buttons on his shirt, letting her tongue play in his crisp black chest hair. She imagined him covered with thick hair in which her fingers would weave in and out creating tiny, ephemeral designs. However he looked would be perfect.

She stood in her underpants, her breasts taut and aching. He turned back to face her. He smiled at her and then yawned. Her knees went weak. She wanted to touch herself, to stroke her breasts, to place the palm of her hand between her thighs, but she didn't dare.

She stretched out on the bed, her legs wide apart. She watched him undress. He neatly folded his shirt and smoothed the corners. He carefully draped his slacks over a chair. At last he came to her, but she was no magnet for him, that much was clear—she was more of an afterthought.

And then in bed, he couldn't make love to her. She nearly wept. She bit her lips so hard they ached. She imagined herself plunging a dagger into her flesh, causing red blood to pour out from between her breasts. She tried to arouse him—she didn't understand why the sight of her, the idea of her, didn't suffice. But it didn't. Finally, she had no choice but to caress herself. She felt embarrassed; not for his failure, but for her own need.

Propped on one elbow, he watched her. His expression was clinical. She threw herself on him and pressed against him. He appeared surprised, but didn't move to embrace her. She lifted her body off his and lay beside him. Her body glistened with perspiration and she shut her eyes to mask her shame.

"I love you," he said then, to her total astonishment. Her eyes opened. "I love you so much," he elaborated in a voice lacking fever. She opened her mouth, but could think of nothing to say. Definitely, she was not in control around this man. He was calling the shots. Her heart hadn't yet stopped its painful pounding, the red flush of the skin at her collarbone had not yet faded, but he was already asleep. Eventually, exhausted, she slept too. And in the morning at breakfast he asked where Sagana had gone.

Rebecca unclenched her fists and let out a long uneven breath. That was all in the past. All that mattered now was her daughter, still asleep in the crib.

She felt herself growing sleepy. She hated to sleep these days, yet she was so often very tired. Sometimes she wished that Lily would stay awake all night and all day. That was cruel, she knew, selfish on her part, hardly the kind of wish an ideal mother would make. But when Lily was asleep, she appeared self-contained, as though she no longer needed Rebecca's care. Perhaps asleep she dreamed of her other mother, the Amazon queen. When Lily slept, the potential for her betrayal of Rebecca was constant. And it was difficult to avoid drifting off into a sympathetic sleep. But with sleep came dreams and she hated her own dreams these days. She had dreams of ebony birds with sharp beaks plucking out her eyes. Sometimes she dreamed of Howard rowing a boat that never moved, and she dreamed about the small town in which they'd landed, where everyone had stared suspiciously at the three of them.

At first, Lily had cried during the bus ride home from the mountain. Rebecca had hoped none of the other passengers were paying attention because from now on all she wanted was to be faceless and nameless. This was what Sagana had taught her, although she knew that this wasn't what Sagana had hoped to teach.

The motion of the bus helped Howard fall asleep. His head fell back onto his seat, but occasionally, as the bus slowed or gained speed, his head dropped onto Rebecca's shoulder. And Lily finally slept in Rebecca's arms, her small body trembling with delicate spasms, one of her hands in a fist. Rebecca remained wide awake, reading highway signs silently, feeling so numb that she stayed in one position for hours. Sometimes the signs seemed to indicate that they were traveling north, other times west, sometimes east: no matter.

She began to feel comfortable with her daughter. It had been gradual. The weight, the warmth of Lily on her lap . . . And then she prayed for the ride to end quickly so that she could take her daughter home with her, where she would keep her safe and secret. Already Howard was a stranger, part of the ugly past. He was

123

not a member of her family, he could never be. She was impatient to be rid of him.

The city would offer her the freedom she now wanted, the freedom to be completely anonymous. In the city nobody would know or care about her, and she and her daughter could live together in privacy. Soon they would move to a new apartment where nobody would ever be able to find them. Not Howard. And not Sagana, if she were alive . . . And Rebecca believed passionately that she was. The idea of the fire consuming the Sagana who had reigned on the mountain was impossible.

They arrived at the bus terminal. First Howard stepped off the bus. Cautiously, Rebecca followed, feeling dazed, holding Lily tightly in her arms. She felt too frightened, though, to leave the tunnel, to step through the gate into the station itself. She remembered how huge it was, how filthy, how crammed with people. Howard pushed her forward, but once inside he appeared as stunned as she was. They stood still, rooted to the floor of the station in front of the gate through which they had entered. Lily was still asleep. "I want to get out of here," Rebecca said, breaking her silence. "I want to go home." Howard didn't reply.

"Home," she repeated, "I want to go home." She started to walk away from Howard, who was still huddled against a wall. He caught up with her.

"What about me?" he asked. The smudges of dirt made an exotic pattern on his face.

"But," she said matter-of-factly, "you can't possibly come with us. No, you can't live with us."

He looked disbelieving, hurt and young and dirty and vulnerable. She continued walking through the station, seeking an exit to the street. He was left standing there, his expression mirroring so many of her own feelings of betrayal.

Rebecca didn't want to remember Howard's expression. She looked over at the crib. If only Lily would awaken soon. She longed to hear Lily cry so that she could comfort her. A lifetime spent convincing her daughter that things were going to be just fine, just perfect . . . that was all she asked. She'd made a decision: nothing would ever induce her to leave her daughter's side again. She was determined to change herself. Radically. One way of life hadn't worked out. Fine. She'd try another.

Sometimes in the mornings as she dressed she would reach for a pair of golden hoop earrings or a necklace of tiny, round pearls or a glittering rhinestone barrette. But she fought this impulse to adorn herself. Finally, she threw them all out—the earrings, the pearls, the barrette. Into the plastic garbage bags along with Lily's soiled plastic diapers. The new Rebecca, Rebecca the perfect mother, had no use for jewelry. Her intentions were no longer to tantalize men. There would be no men from now on in her life. Her only lover was to be her daughter, who was the most desirable lover of all. She should have realized that long ago.

Most mornings she just hastily ran a brush through her hair, patted water on her face, and never allowed her own glance to linger too long in the mirror. A perfect mother possessed no vanity about herself, only about her child. She deliberately wore old blue jeans, work shirts, and sneakers. She discarded lacy blouses, leather slacks, and pointed shoes.

Not leaving Lily's side meant not returning to waitressing, of course. Money would have to be gotten

some other way. She could not bear the idea of someone else watching her child, even for a few hours while
she earned a living, even if the baby were asleep and
didn't know that temporarily she was gone. She was
sure that Lily would know at once, would immediately
sense the abandonment and would never forgive her.
This life wouldn't be easy, but she was determined to
live it.

At last Lily did awake. With a small whisper at first,
perhaps just a sigh, and Rebecca was instantly at the
side of the sturdy wooden crib in which Lily lay on her
back in her violet terrycloth pajamas with pompoms on
the feet. Lily rubbed her eyes with two balled fists. Suddenly she smiled brightly and began watching her
mother, her big blue eyes as alert and watchful as a
detective's. This lasted a minute, and then her face
crumpled and the smile was replaced by a frown, her
pink lips compressing and twisting like a rubber band.
She began to cry. Rebecca, knowing that she was hungry, held out her hands and Lily quickly grabbed them,
still crying. Lifting her up in her arms, Rebecca carried
her into the kitchen, singing soothing nonsense syllables
like any perfect mother would. Expertly, she opened
the refrigerator door, removed the baby's bottle from
the top shelf, and closed the door gently, while balancing Lily on one arm. Other than Lily's bottles, the refrigerator was almost empty: a few carrots turning soft
in an open plastic bag, a rusty head of lettuce, a small
bottle of apple juice. Rebecca had little interest in eating; not because she was watching her weight as she
used to, but because she was now solely concerned with
Lily's appetite. All that mattered was that the baby be
fed well, that the baby be pudgy and soft and smiling.
Lily grabbed for her bottle. Her lips encircled the nip-

ple. She sucked. Her forehead grew smooth, her eyes closed. Rebecca strolled into the living room. Lily, in her arms, still sucked from the bottle. Rebecca settled on the sofa.

Since their return from the mountain, Rebecca had read book after book on how to care for babies. She read when Lily was asleep. She picked the books off the rack at the pharmacy. There seemed to be an endless supply. Naturally, all of the books had photographs of babies on their covers, and usually the babies were blonde and blue-eyed with rosy cheeks, like Lily. Usually they were laughing. Sometimes there were photographs of mothers as well—holding the babies or sitting alertly nearby. The mothers, always brunettes, were young and pretty and appeared confident. Their lips were always posed carefully in Mona Lisa smiles. Rebecca found herself studying the mothers' faces, seeking further clues to the whole mystery, to the perfection of the role. She had gone so far as to memorize whole passages from these books. One of her favorites, which she sometimes recited out loud to Lily, was:

> Cooperation, not discipline, is the key word with babies. If you cooperate when she needs you, she'll be more likely to cooperate when you tell her not to do something.

Lily pushed the bottle aside. She was satisfied.

Rebecca had been stunned to discover that Lily, sometime during her life on the mountain, had begun to crawl. The first time that Lily insisted on twisting free of Rebecca and moving on her own, Rebecca felt betrayed yet one more time, but only momentarily, deciding that it just showed what a strong and determined child she'd given birth to.

Now Rebecca placed Lily on the rug. Lily took off immediately. She moved her arms in alternating strokes, left-right, left-right, a swimmer on land. Lily always crawled in a straight line to Rebecca's bedroom. Rebecca walked alongside.

Her bedroom had changed. The double bed was now made up with a plain grey blanket. Once she'd used only frilly, flowery covers, but no more. The red satin sheets had been shoved somewhere in the bottom of a drawer. And Lily had a new crib, with painted peacocks on the side and a jangly mobile of birds and clowns and fish fastened along the top. The mobile was the only decoration in the room. Rebecca had taken down everything on the walls from the old days—all the photographs of herself in various sensual poses. Now the walls were bare except for one oval mirror which Rebecca didn't care to use herself, but in front of which she held her child. Lily, thinking that another baby was in front of her, grew happy and played with her mirror image.

But Lily, in an abrupt change of pattern, did not enter the familiar bedroom world. Cooing and swimming, the violet pajamas now slapping against the floor, she continued down the dim hallway and stopped at the end, right outside the door to Sagana's room. Eagerly, she looked up at her mother.

"No," said Rebecca.

Lily brushed at the door.

"No! You can't " Rebecca lifted her daughter from the floor. Lily began to cry. Rebecca felt torn: she couldn't bear to cause Lily unhappiness. But she would not open that door. Lily twisted and turned in her arms.

Rebecca stared at the closed door. She could clearly see the room as it had been.

It was an ordinary room, nothing like the royal hut on the mountain. Sagana slept on a narrow bed which she made up during the day with a black quilted comforter. There was a chest of drawers and a wooden desk. There was no mirror in the room. On top of the desk was a framed photograph of the two of them as children, Rebecca in a short pink dress, Sagana in a blue dress down past her knees; Rebecca with a smile that was intended to please, Sagana with a sour, suspicious expression, her eyeglasses glinting and crooked. It had been taken by Arnie before the staircase incident. He'd just received the camera as a gift. "Cheese," he shouted in the schoolyard where the girls posed during recess hour. Sagana initially protested but was finally persuaded to pose by Rebecca. Rebecca could have gone on all day, could have posed for four more rolls of film, but Arnie moved on, eager to photograph his friends. "This photo is titled," Sagana announced out of the blue one day not long before she left, "Tits and Ms. Ass."

Lily grew still. A few tears left smudges on her face, but she looked content again, the room behind the closed door forgotten.

Rebecca picked up her daughter and backed away from the room. She stared at the door as though a ghost might pop out. Maybe Sagana had been hiding in there all along, waiting for precisely this moment. Maybe she had returned home from the mountain before Rebecca. Not until she was all the way back at the entrance of the living room did Rebecca breathe easily and turn around. Lily stared into her mother's eyes.

# 19

It was time, Rebecca decided, to take Lily out for her daily walk. She resented these excursions because Lily seemed almost to become public property. So many people stared at her and smiled and winked and stopped for a better look. It was a new side of New York to Rebecca: strangers coming alive in this way, showing their . . . what was it? . . . maternal side, she supposed. Even the men who stopped to gaze at the baby seemed more like women, their faces becoming soft and tender. But Lily was going to remain a healthy baby, and that meant taking her outside. Anyway, Lily loved being outdoors. She glowed. She loved being wheeled along the city streets in her stroller or being carried high on Rebecca's back in her blue canvas carrier. Rebecca was growing strong from the weight of Lily, although sometimes the back carrier caused her emotional discomfort: feeling Lily, but not seeing her. It was a tenuous connection in a way. What if some crazy person came up from behind, reached in, scooped Lily out, stole her? Any crazy street person was likely to do that—or an emissary from Sagana. But the back carrier allowed her to take Lily places the stroller couldn't go.

She walked carefully, nervous about jostling Lily. One foot in front of the other in a straight line . . . In the past she had walked these same streets less carefully, a different Rebecca playing a different role . . .

She and Evan had been taking a walk together. Rebecca loved strolling idly with Evan because it made her feel as though they were truly a couple in love. But then, as she always did during such strolls, she started coveting the skirts and hats and jackets and jewelry in the shop windows. "I really must have a new pair of shoes," she remembered saying to Evan, and the memory of the sound of her own voice shamed her: so petulant, so demanding. If Evan really loved her, she believed, he would eagerly buy her shoes, gloves, earrings . . . anything her heart desired, anything to add to her beauty. Anything to please her. They went into shoe store after shoe store. At least twenty pairs of shoes were discarded before she found the perfect pair. She stood, Cinderella contented at last. She gazed at herself in the mirror. These were the only shoes for her . . . that day. They were white satin, with small heels curved like graceful waves. Of course now she felt she needed a new dress to match the shoes, also white, but not virginal, something exotic, white with peacock feathers and beads, low-cut and tight. Evan would surely want to take her out on the town once he'd seen her wearing the complete outfit. She envisioned the pleasure on his face when he saw her all dressed up.

On the way home, Evan suggested that they stop for ice cream. In the ice cream parlour, she grew convinced that he was eyeing their waitress, a tall blonde in a slinky white leotard top and a white skirt slit up her thigh. Rebecca changed her mind and decided to buy herself a splashy red dress instead of white.

The waitress bent over their table. Yes, Rebecca was absolutely certain that Evan was staring directly at the waitress's breasts. Through the thin white material of the waitress's leotard, her large round nipples were clearly defined. Rebecca was afraid to look at Evan. She averted her eyes and frowned. Her shoulders were suddenly so tense that they hurt.

Evan sat across from her, eating his hot fudge sundae with precise finicky gestures. She couldn't even touch her own single scoop of vanilla. Pushing it away, she stared once again at the waitress who was now waiting on another table. Evan followed her stare. The waitress, as though sensing their interest, looked up. She ignored Rebecca and smiled widely at the appreciative Evan. Then she returned her attention to her new customers. "Sprinkles and cherries on top?" she asked in a breathy voice. "Yes, lots of cherries," laughed one of the customers, a middle-aged man in a wrinkled suit.

"I'm prettier than she is," Rebecca said loudly, not caring if the waitress or her customers heard—or, for that matter, if the whole ice cream parlor and all of Broadway heard. Although she adored it when men fantasized about her as she waited on them, her man was not going to do that about another waitress.

"Of course," replied Evan, licking his spoon with a measured and swift dart of his tongue, "of course you are."

"Don't placate me," she grumbled. "You desire her."

"Only you," Evan had insisted. "I desire only you." He stared at her intensely. Rebecca felt mollified: it was herself that was reflected back to her in his eyes. The waitress's reflection was nowhere.

"Let's go," he said huskily.

She nodded, thinking that for dramatic effect she'd come to him in bed wearing nothing but the new white satin shoes.

Car horns were honking. Rebecca looked around. She was standing still, with Lily on her back, in the middle of the street. Lost in reverie, she'd begun to cross against the light. They could have been killed. Lily was crying, frightened by all the noise. Damn the past! The past didn't count. All that counted was Lily's safety. "I'm sorry," she said under her breath to the drivers of the cars. She hurried back to the curb. "I'm sorry," she said to Lily for abruptly ending their walk like this. Now all she wanted was to get Lily back home, fast.

Upstairs, she played with Lily for a long time. She snapped a series of photographs of her: Lily studying a wrinkle in the rug; Lily giggling; Lily being bathed; and finally in her crib asleep.

Rebecca sat down heavily on her bed. She removed her shoes and stretched out her legs. She lay down. In order to be a perfect mother she had to walk a straight line. She had to avoid unpleasant thoughts, unpleasant memories. It was her responsibility.

She opened her eyes. She must have fallen asleep fully dressed. She continued to lay still, treasuring this awakening from a dreamless sleep. What a joy it was not to have dreamt of Sagana, Evan, and Howard. She didn't feel at all groggy. Soon she would tiptoe to the crib to check on her daughter . . . but not quite yet. She was enjoying this pleasant awakening; it was so unfamiliar. But then she heard a soft cry from the crib. She stood. She stretched her arms toward the ceiling. Softly, she padded over to peer into the crib.

Immediately she panicked. Lily was not awake at all. The cry had been imaginary. She was sleeping with her small face pressed firmly down against the mattress. Every one of the infant care books had warned mothers about the danger of suffocation! The books described the horrors of the baby silently choking, of the baby gasping for air, of the mother who didn't respond. She turned the baby over. How unyielding Lily's flesh felt. Lily was now on her back. Rebecca stared at the powder that had attached itself to her daughter's lips during the night. There must have been some stray powder on the mattress. A kind of talcum powder? Or some harmless dust? A wet powder, more like a foam. A bloody foam, she now saw, not talc or pollen.

Rebecca sought out Lily's eyes for a clue to what had happened. Lily's eyes were open wide and were as blue as ever, but they were hazed. Lifting the child in her arms, she shook her, but there was no response. This was a doll, not Lily! Sagana, Rhea, someone, had entered during the night and kidnapped her flesh and blood child and had left this perverse look-alike, this Lily-doll in her place. Another mocking doll.

She felt like a doll herself. How could one doll coax life from another? It was impossible. Dolls were destined to be forever lifeless. Why bother shaking a toy, why bother trying to make it breathe?

She screamed. She sat primly on the edge of her bed. She unbuttoned her blouse, baring both breasts. Immediately her nipples hardened. She placed Lily's cold still lips to her breast. Lily would suck and suck and swallow, growing newly strong and energetic. For the first time since Lily's birth, she would offer her food from within her own body.

Rebecca hummed a lullaby to the lifeless child, the child she could neither fathom nor accept as dead. Lily's lips stayed closed.

Her nipple turned inward and grew soft. She massaged it with her finger into a point once again, then opened Lily's cold lips with her thumb and index fingers, stretching them as wide as they would go. She placed Lily's open mouth against her erect nipple. But still the baby refused to nurse at the breast. Rebecca stared down at the rounded shapes of both of her breasts; suddenly they were repulsive, obscene.

And at last she understood how much she had come to love Lily. A love unlike any other she'd known. The loss of Lily was like the loss of her own life. Did Sagana, wherever she was, love Diana as much? Had Sagana lost Diana, too, back on the mountain?

Rebecca also understood that in every possible way she had failed. She had lost. Not merely one battle, but the whole pathetic war. All was lost. Lily was dead, and she and Sagana remained alive. She was more certain than ever that Sagana had survived the fire.

She washed her daughter's entire body. When Lily was pink and glowing, Rebecca opened the top bureau drawer and removed a dress for her to wear, a frilly dress with pink roses and lilac butterflies on a white background. She'd purchased it for Lily only a few days before, saving it for a special occasion. She slipped the lacy dress over Lily's head. Then she propped Lily up and combed her hair with a small delicate comb.

Her keys were in her pants pocket. She had money for the subway. She walked to the subway station, cradling Lily in her arms. Placing the token in the turnstile slot, she pushed her way through, whispering comforting words to Lily. She hoped Lily wasn't frightened by the subway station. On the platform, she leaned against a worn hair spray advertisement that was stuck to the wall.

She heard before she saw it, the train pulling into the station, and then watched as the men and women began their massive surge forward, pushing their way on. Venturing only slightly forward, she and Lily were imme-

135

diately caught up and propelled inside. The car was packed tightly and Rebecca held onto a pole, cradling Lily with her free arm. After several stops, the sign announcing the station that was her destination appeared through the subway car windows.

She was taking Lily back to the hospital in which she'd been born. She wanted the doctor who had delivered her to see her again, to heal her, to bring her back to life.

The hospital seemed unfamiliar. She went to the information desk and stood on line. Her turn came. The receptionist was looking down at a blank piece of paper, her pen poised in the air. She waited, but Rebecca had no words. No words could convey what she needed to convey. She said nothing, holding Lily's cold hand in her own.

The receptionist looked up. Rebecca took hold of the receptionist's slim hand, which trembled, and placed it on Lily's lips. A male guard stationed nearby ran over, ready to rescue the receptionist; Rebecca turned to him and tried to grasp his hand in order to allow him, too, to feel her daughter's cool flesh. But he resisted her violently. He pushed her off the line and then continued to push her forward. Rebecca was not sorry that he had taken command of the situation. She hoped that he was taking her to see the doctor.

She held Lily tightly to her chest as the guard pushed her forward. Was he taking her to the one doctor who could help her? The doctor would provide her with an answer, and then there would be no more questions. The guard placed her in a room. He shut the door. Rebecca kissed Lily's forehead as she waited. The door of the room opened. The guard had returned, accompanied now by a tall man in a suit and tie. Rebecca

136

knew at once that he was the doctor. Even though he didn't look exactly as she remembered him. He was definitely the one. He lifted both of his strong, well-manicured hands and spread his palms. His voice was deep: "Give me the child."

Rebecca immediately offered her child. He held Lily in his arms. He stared at her and took one of her little hands in his own. He let the hand drop. He looked up at Rebecca, his face impassive. "This is not your fault," he declared, enunciating each word with precision. "There was no warning. Nothing could have prevented this. It isn't your fault. Get hold of yourself. You're still young," he smiled. "You can have more children. Calm down. We'll call your husband. You must learn to cope and go on with your life as before. Remember, this is not your fault."

Rebecca stared at him, nodding as he spoke. She very much wanted to be a good pupil. She wanted him to be impressed by how quickly she understood.

"Well then," the doctor said, glancing at the clock on the wall, "now you must make arrangements . . ."

Rebecca could feel herself standing up, then falling. Her legs were giving way. She couldn't stop herself. Then someone's arms were supporting her. She was lifted up in someone's arms, and she hoped that she might leave the earth beneath her feet forever.

# 20

Rebecca didn't recognize where she was. Everything around her was vague. It took long moments for her to begin to discern shapes and colors, and then finally to realize that she was back inside her own apartment. She felt no sense of joy, no sense of a warm homecoming. She was lying on an unmade bed. Her own narrow one, of course. The one in which she slept nightly. Then why did it feel unnatural beneath her? Her body was bathed in perspiration. Her eyes were crusty. Lifting her arm required extreme effort. She forced herself to raise one arm high enough so that she could feel her own wet forehead. She must have had another fever. She half expected to see Howard Geller sitting before her in his faded overalls, braiding his leather straps and smirking. But he wasn't here. Not this time. This time she seemed to be very much alone. She stared at her hand. Judging by how bony her wrist looked, she'd lost a good deal of weight; it was nearly skeletal.

And there . . . what was that large object standing so close to her, seeming to tower so high? Lily's crib. She moaned. She was no longer a mother! Lily was dead. Which meant without life, without breath. Which meant that she existed no longer as Rebecca, the mother of Lily. But what then did she exist as? Her daughter had died. The doctor had told her so. Someone else must have buried her, since she couldn't recall anything more. Lily was not alive. A complete stranger must have been the last person to touch her daughter.

She wept. But her tears were useless. She was no

longer Lily's mother. Her tears dried, and she cursed instead. She cursed the doctor, the hospital guard, the subway, the earth itself . . . Most of all she cursed Sagana.

Sagana had declared war on her the day she had taken Lily and run off. Or had it happened even before that? When had the war between them begun? No matter when it began. It was war. And so she would become a fighter. She would fight for Lily. It really wasn't too late to do that. For Lily's memory. For Lily's honor. She owed Lily that much.

Once again she would change. She'd be renewed. She no longer felt weak. She felt strong and energetic. Even as Lily's mother, she'd never felt so alive. This was different. This was special. The fever had vanished. She felt almost buoyant. Nobody had cared for her this time: not Sagana, not Howard Geller. And so it was clear that she would need nobody else now.

She sat up. Placing the palms of her hands to her face, she touched her forehead, her eyes, her lips. These eyes had gazed upon Lily, these lips had kissed her daughter's skin over and over again. Her own face, yes. But different. She felt more like a jungle animal, less like a woman. Animals didn't feel worthless or ashamed of themselves; they simply were. They didn't know self-doubt. Animals did, however, hunt. She ran her finger along her teeth. Animals hunted in order to survive, and she would too. She would hunt and strike and capture and feast upon her prey, and her prey would be Sagana. Sagana was also, she was sure, looking to hunt her down. But she would surprise her. She would strike first. What a fine exhilarating way to feel. A very fine way to feel. She wiped the perspiration from her brow and neck and underarms, eager to cleanse herself, to become the queen of the jungle.

An ice-cold shower would be next. Not exactly the kind of treatment a doctor would recommend following a fever, but she would have no use for doctors from now on. In the jungle there was no room for modern medicine; after all, her daughter had died and the doctor in the modern hospital had been unable to save her.

She stood effortlessly and savored the feeling of standing tall beside her bed. From now on she would learn to be her own healer. She would rely upon her own animal instinct for survival. And in this way, like a feline roaming freely, she would relish and delight in the present tense, life itself, her own breath from moment to moment. She would not brood about the past.

Barefoot, she walked through the apartment to the bathroom, refusing to look left or right, refusing to see the scattered toys, the half-used box of plastic diapers, the never-opened can of baby food, the one little white shoe. She would not break down again and weep for Lily. Animal mothers loved their young, and so had she, but they didn't collapse, faint, mourn—and neither would she, ever again.

The water ran all over her body, making her feel even stronger. The cold was startling and invigorating. She examined this new angular body and decided that it definitely appealed to her. It would be easy to grow swift and cunning and agile. Sagana had always been bony. They would be more evenly matched this way.

The yellow bar of soap fell from her hands, and as she bent to retrieve it she remembered something. A moment from childhood. She and Sagana playing in the bathtub together some afternoon. They were sitting in the water at opposite ends. The game consisted of passing the soap back and forth and never losing it, never allowing it to sink to the bottom of the tub. Eventually, the soap somehow always landed on the tub's bottom, and one of them gained a point. Ten points meant you'd lost, and the game would start again. It was an old reliable game, one they liked to play in the afternoon when Saggie's parents were gone. But this time, instead of sailing the soap back to Sagana as she was supposed to, Rebecca held onto it.

"You can't have it, you can't have it," she sang.

Sagana, rising to the bait, attacked her. They were both laughing. They wrestled for the soap; they were slippery and giddy. Finally, Sagana snatched it. Gasping for breath from so much laughter, she started to crawl off with it back to her side of the tub. Rebecca grasped for the soap once more, and they wrestled and laughed again until the soap fell between them right to the tub's bottom and just sat there, a yellow stone. Together, they reached to retrieve it, but somehow Rebecca's hand touched and remained nestled for a moment in the soft spot between Sagana's legs. Rebecca's hand felt charged and jolted as though by electricity. Sagana stopped laughing. Startled, they forgot the soap and stared at each other . . .

Rebecca turned off the cold water. She blinked and ran her fingers through her long wet hair to untangle it. Her heart was racing. Animals did not, she reminded herself as she furiously toweled herself dry, remember. Anything. There were no haunting pasts constantly revealing themselves, constantly frightening them.

Out of the shower . . . walking nude and wet around the apartment, she left wet footprints. She looked sharply around, now noting everything. The big pink rubber ball Lily loved to grasp with both of her arms, the violet terrycloth pajamas carelessly left on the sofa. The box of diapers, the tumbling Humpty Dumpty toy with its enormous turquoise eyes, the flamboyant jingling mobile that hung above the wooden crib with the peacocks painted on the sides. Rebecca roamed back and forth concentrating on these things. As she walked, she grew more and more accustomed to the feel of her new skinny body, her childless body. A decision had to be made, and it would be better to make it now, immediately. She couldn't put it off. She couldn't go on living, not even for another day, surrounded by these reminders of Lily.

She found a clean pair of slacks and a blouse. She was pleased at the way they hung, too loose now for her slender body.

The first thing to be gotten rid of would be the crib. It had been the place of death. This was the first moment to test her new vitality and determination. She would have to lift the large wooden crib from the floor. Just as she expected, she had an unprecedented amount of strength. It wasn't at all difficult to lift it up and to carry it into the hallway and then down the flights of stairs to the street. She didn't bother waiting for the elevator.

The fresh air and sudden daylight were shocking and invigorating. She carried the large crib to the corner of the block, where she deposited it. Then she turned around and headed toward the building without looking back.

In a kind of fury she opened drawers, pulling out bibs and pajamas and little socks. Then she went through the apartment, finding all the toys and all the photographs. She threw everything into two plastic trash bags. She tied the tops of the bags into knots, and with

142

one bulging black bag in each hand, she repeated her journey into the hallway, down the flights of stairs and to the corner of the block. Defiantly, she held her chin out, looking at nobody. Slowly she walked home this time, treasuring the feeling of having come to life. Alive, yes. Ready to do battle.

Sitting down on her narrow bed, she closed her eyes: she would not be sleeping here much longer. Another apartment would soon become her home, and from there, from her new headquarters, she would declare and wage her own war of vengeance upon Sagana. She would fight to win, to savor the spicy taste of victory.

# 21

Before the sun was up she'd risen and showered, again delighting in the feel of cold water on her body. Brushing her teeth, she was tempted to bare them as a ferocious animal would. Today she was going hunting: not for food, but for shelter. Ordinarily, apartment hunting in the city was difficult and tedious. But this time it was going to be easy. Her needs were simple now. A jungle animal didn't need to worry about safe blocks, safe buildings.

She rode down in the elevator with a teenaged boy, Howard's age. But this boy had short blonde hair and wore a starched white shirt and a red tie. Nothing like Howard. She closed her eyes and Lily was with her, pushing the buttons to every floor and laughing. She opened her eyes. The elevator stopped and the boy held the door open for her. She strode past, not even thanking him.

She knew exactly how she intended to go about the hunt. First, she was going to head downtown on the subway, and then she was going to head as far east as possible. Somewhere along the way she'd pick up a copy of a newspaper and she'd look at the ads for the cheapest, smallest apartments on the east side. Way downtown.

On the subway she leaned against the pole, her back rigid. It was a long ride. The car was nearly empty but she stood rather than sat. The few other passengers didn't look at her and she didn't look at them. She didn't care about them. This was how life should be lived.

Downtown, she walked along blocks that once would have struck terror in her, but no more. She bought a newspaper and turned immediately to the back to find the apartment ads. She skimmed until she found one—very cheap, very far east. She took off, ignoring the panhandlers and the winos all asking for change. She grew exuberant with each step. The streets were dirty and noisy and she was happy with her hunt.

The apartment was already home, although she'd only been living in it for a few days. She'd set up a spare sort of housekeeping. On some hooks in a closet she hung a pair of blue jeans and a few shirts. Her underwear was stuffed into one of the two bureau drawers. She brought no dishes or silverware because of the memories associated with each plate, each fork, each knife . . . the lasagna dinner that Sagana had once cooked for her; the knife Evan always preferred to use . . .

One of the first things she did in her new home was to stand over the bathroom sink with a scissors in one hand and her long hair in the other. With bold decisive strokes and no mirror to guide her, she cut and cut. Each time a large spidery clump fell into the basin she felt relieved, sensing that she was getting closer to her essence, her wild animal self. Touching her scalp with her hands, she was at last satisfied: what was left of her hair was stark and short, without shape.

She stared out of the only window, which faced directly into a window in the building opposite. Its shades were drawn, reminding her that this was one more way for her to insulate herself, to cut herself off. Tugging at the faded grey shade on her own window, she finally pulled it halfway down. In its center, like a bull's-eye, was a hole which had been taped over. The black tape was in the shape of a cross. With one final, ferocious tug, the shade came all the way down to the dirty sill. A victory, even one as small as this, pleased her.

Tonight she had big plans for herself. Tonight she was going to plan her revenge. She arranged herself uncomfortably on the edge of the bed as though she were doing penance of some sort. Feet flat on the floor, spine rigid, breathing deeply. It was imperative that she confront Sagana. This was all that was left for her to live for. She had to see her face to face, in the flesh, in order to wreak vengeance upon her. Sagana, the betrayer, would now be betrayed.

But how? How to act, how to make her move . . . She was certain that Sagana had returned to New York. She knew that Sagana was too smart, too self-protective, to let a mere fire destroy her. And she knew that Sagana would come back. New York was her home. And it was where Rebecca would be.

But how could she locate Sagana and where would they meet? Not on Sagana's turf, wherever that was. Rebecca almost laughed at the thought of Sagana now living in one of those proper residences for women. Or maybe Sagana now lived on the streets, a shopping bag in each hand. Maybe the best meeting place would be her own turf . . . her new home. Why not? She would bring Sagana to her. Let Sagana see her in her new living quarters. Let Sagana see that she was not afraid of filth and decay, that she no longer demanded high ceilings and spacious closets, that she no longer used scented soaps and oils. Somehow she would beckon Sagana, entice her, lead her on . . . And then she would attack. The specific plans of the attack would have to come later. First she had to contact Sagana.

She sat for hours, her hands folded, keeping her

spine as straight as a ruler. She had to find a way to reach Sagana. At last she bowed her head, relaxed her back. She blinked back tears. She didn't know how. Sagana was free within the huge, crowded city. Before, she had always known where Sagana was. It was unthinkable that Sagana was lost to her.

She ran her hands through her short hair and stood. She went to the window. Again the shade was resistant, but this time she wanted it up. She tugged and pushed until it rose. Outside, dawn was nearing and she still didn't have her answer. She looked down and thought about jumping, about her own death.

Her neighbor across the way had his shade up too and she could see him. How strange that someone else was up at this hour. His back was to her but she could see that he was a slim young man reading a newspaper at a table. He didn't seem to sense her gaze. Rebecca smiled; she had her answer. The newspaper. Through the Personals, just like Sagana. She would place an ad, and Sagana, humbled, would read it and would respond. Rebecca would dictate all the terms. This time Sagana would not be Queen.

What should the notice say? She wanted Sagana to read it and to understand immediately who it was from. It should both enrage and entice her. She couldn't just say, SAGANA: MEET ME. REBECCA, since there were others who also might have returned safely from the mountain, others who also might have escaped the blaze. She didn't want any of them to become involved. Not Rhea, for instance. Or Mara.

Should she also solicit new members to join her in an idyllic colony? COME TOGETHER IN A PARADISE! Or should she be more direct, leaving mimicking aside . . . Should she fully express her anger, her rage . . . MUR-

147

DERER OF MY CHILD! YOU WILL SOON MEET YOUR FATE! Or should she be bland, emotionless, and state simply, S: R WISHES TO SEE YOU. Or the trick possibility, the lie: S: I AM SO SORRY. FORGIVE. R.

Which?

She was a fearless hunter and so she'd act boldly in a big way. She'd do it all. She'd print all four of the ads. She'd mimic, she'd display her anger, she'd show her distance, she'd parade her deceit. And Sagana would be thrown completely off balance. All Sagana would be able to know for certain was that Rebecca was contacting her. She would not be certain why. She wouldn't know what to expect.

Rebecca paused only long enough to throw on a jacket. She would be waiting at the newspaper offices when they opened the doors, and her four personal ads would appear in the very next edition. Racing down the stairs of her building, one more thing came to her; after each message she would add one brief line: YOU WILL RESPOND. It was a command that definitely would be obeyed.

# 22

The paper came out on Wednesday. Before dawn, she'd already showered and eaten a large breakfast of bacon, eggs, and muffins. Then she paced throughout the tiny apartment. Back and forth. She was so hungry. She felt insatiable. Nothing would ever be enough to satisfy her. Would she ever feel full again? In a way, she loved feeling this hunger, this need. She paced, ate crackers and fruits, paced, then ate bread and hunks of cheese.

She was waiting until the dilapidated newsstand a block away opened for business, but she could wait no longer and ran downstairs, arriving before the owner had rolled up the shutters. She shifted from foot to foot, still hungry. She envisioned the way her messages would look in print, and she envisioned thick pancakes and waffles drenched in syrup. Finally the newsstand opened.

She turned to the Personals page. There they were . . . Her very own messages. They were spread out on the page, which produced an effect that she liked. Between each of her notices were announcements of dance contests, overeaters groups, and sexual therapies. Spread out this way, Sagana would be forced to look even harder.

COME TOGETHER IN A PARADISE!

MURDERER OF MY CHILD! YOU WILL SOON MEET YOUR FATE!

S: R WISHES TO SEE YOU.

S: I AM SO SORRY. FORGIVE. R.

Upstairs again, she reread her messages inside her doorway. She closed the door and read them again. And again. All day long she read them, pacing and eating. She ate cans of tuna fish and slices of roast beef and whole loaves of bread. Reading, pacing, eating: she felt excited. Sagana would come to her. Sagana would feel her power. Sagana would be sorry! Rebecca would win. Rebecca could not be blamed for . . . anything.

The newspaper came out only once a week. She would have to wait until the following week for Sagana's response. That Sagana would read her ads and respond she had no doubt.

At last, the following Wednesday arrived. Again she was the first to buy a copy of the newspaper. And again, she couldn't wait to get upstairs. Right there she skimmed through the paper until she came to the Personals. And there! The fifth message from the top was clearly a response to one of hers. I DID NOT MURDER HIM, it read, IT WAS YOUR FATHER. She laughed aloud. Delightful! Someone else, some stranger, had also responded to her message. Obviously she and Sagana were not the only two souls engaged in war.

There was, however, no response from Sagana. Reading the pages over and over convinced her of this. But she no longer felt anxious. She felt that she had all the time in the world to wait. She didn't doubt that Sagana had read her messages and would respond. Her revenge was not going to be denied her. Sagana was deliberately making her wait, thinking Rebecca would panic. Well, how little—after all these years—she knew her friend, her former friend.

The following Wednesday she broke the pattern: she slept late and awoke slowly, arriving at the newsstand long after it had opened. She sensed victory and she was savoring the anticipation. Slowly, she walked back to her building. Slowly she climbed the stairs. Inside, she casually placed the paper down and made herself a sandwich, which she ate before sitting down to read. She yawned. She skimmed the paper, looking at advertisements for hair salons and Japanese beds. The Personals page . . . languidly, she began to read.

The spell was broken. Sagana had given in. She'd responded once to each of Rebecca's messages.

DON'T DELUDE YOURSELF. YOU SHATTER DREAMS.

I DO NOT ALLOW OTHERS TO DICTATE MY FATE.

I, TOO, WISH TO SEE YOU.

AT LAST YOU ARE SORRY, BUT PERHAPS IT IS TOO LATE.

Sagana was in New York. Sagana was alive. Sagana had read her ads and had responded. Rebecca read and reread the page. But each time, something disturbed her. Another ad. This ad was not from Sagana and yet she knew that it was meant for her.

MY TWO FRIENDS, YOU CAN'T SIMPLY FORGET ME, YOU KNOW. I WAS THERE TOO. I COUNT TOO, DON'T I?

Damn Howard! Here he was again, butting in. Her head began to ache. Sighing, she opened her refrigerator and removed a fatty steak. She would broil it and eat it rare: she'd begun to like it barely cooked, red and chewy.

Replies from both of them. She'd succeeded. Succeeded! Both of them would come to her. Originally she'd only wanted Sagana, but it was okay—no, it was perfect—that Howard would also come.

But first she had one more task. She had to place one final ad. Stating a time and place. No more than that. But that would be enough. She'd decided on the meeting place. It would be Washington Square Park. She and Saggie had loved to visit the park when they were younger. Throughout high school they went there after school to listen to the folk singers and poets.

They would all meet beneath the arch. She would make it late on a Saturday when it would be dark, with a feeling of danger in the air.

# 23

Saturday morning. Where had the boundless energy gone, the insatiable animal appetite? She was sapped of all energy, all strength. Yet she would not succumb to this lethargy. She could not allow fear or doubt into her mind. She was determined to go through with her plan. Tonight, she would force herself to meet Sagana and Howard beneath the arch in Washington Square. She had waited so long for this. Nothing else counted. Her world was narrow, but it was hers. She would try to enlist Howard as an ally against Sagana. Or perhaps she wouldn't bother. Perhaps she would turn against him as well. And upon Sagana, there was no doubt she'd wreak revenge.

What kind of revenge? How? All day she lay listlessly in bed. She had no ideas and she was unable to rouse herself. But when the sun set she shivered and came alive. Her nostrils expanded as she inhaled the odor—present even inside her stuffy apartment—of the nighttime. Jumping up, she was now all nerve endings, ready, ready . . . Daytime had been the calm before the storm. With the nighttime she was the storm itself.

Dressing in an instant, she threw on yesterday's clothes. Red pants and a white T-shirt, both too large for her. Her short spiked hair didn't need to be combed.

Sagana would weep. Sagana would be powerless. She'd be lost and subdued, broken in spirit, broken at last. And Howard would understand that he was just a boy, powerless against Rebecca.

Rebecca raced down the filthy flights of stairs. Soaring along the streets, seeing and absorbing nothing, she was immune to the life and spirit of the city. She was moving fast. Nothing, nothing would interfere as she decisively neared her prey.

And just then something interrupted her. It was something she noticed, despite herself, out of the corner of her eye, and it brought her completely up short. Took her totally by surprise. It was startling. First the colors entered her consciousness. Then the colors took shape and emerged as a multi-colored bird inside of a large intricately wrought cage.

Almost involuntarily, she drew herself closer. Unlike the black birds on the mountain, this bird's feathers were scarlet and aqua and silver. Rebecca stood close to it, separated only by the glass of the pet store window. Her breathing misted the window. The bird cocked its head and stared back at her. Its ebony eye was both accusatory and compelling.

She felt frightened. She was a jungle animal with no time for this, no time to gaze at pretty birds. But this bird wasn't merely pretty. Something much more. That accusatory eye. It made her catch her breath. Her heart raced. The bird was a reminder of something . . . something which she'd been blocking out for so long. She wouldn't give in. Not now. She would not remember! She refused to remember. Something about herself. And about Sagana. And Evan. There was nothing she could do. The angle of its beak, the shape of its feathers . . . like that bird she had once touched. . . Now of all times, the worst possible time, because this bird . . . was shaped exactly like the birthmark on Sagana's hip. And then the images, the whole scene flooded her mind . . .

Evan opened the apartment door. Inside, Sagana was sitting on the sofa, talking on the phone. Actually, she seemed to be in the process of hurriedly hanging up the phone. She was barefoot and wearing her black flannel pajamas—the button-down top and the pull-on pants with an elastic waist. Her expression was strange. She looked embarrassed at having been discovered on the phone.

"Who was that?" Rebecca asked from the doorway.

"A wrong number."

"Oh?" Evan said, shutting the door behind them but not moving away from the doorway.

Sagana curled her legs up and rested her chin on her knees. "A very talky wrong number," she elaborated. "You know, Becky, like that man who was calling a fish store but fell in love with you over the phone."

Rebecca giggled. She must have misinterpreted Sagana's expression. It must not have been embarrassment. Anyway, Sagana's expression didn't matter because she had something else on her mind. After they had left the ice cream parlor, Evan had gone into a liquor store and emerged with two large bottles of tequila. "We," he pronounced solemnly as they walked toward Rebecca's apartment, "are going to have a tequila evening tonight."

They'd never had a tequila evening before, although Evan had supplied her with vodka evenings, gin evenings, brandy evenings. . . On the nights they drank gin, she thought of the Roaring Twenties and imagined herself a provocative flapper in a glittering fringed dress with strands of beads around her neck. On vodka evenings she became a haughty but sensual Russian in furs and emeralds. Maybe tonight she'd be a coffee-colored

Latin beauty in a ruffled peasant blouse that was constantly slipping off one shoulder . . .

She and Evan, standing together in the doorway, were soon going to be embraced in tequila love. So Sagana's expression didn't matter in the slightest.

But then Evan left her in the doorway, left her standing there and crossed inside the apartment and sat down on the sofa next to Sagana. He crossed his legs and appeared to be making himself comfortable, as though he had no intention of going anywhere for a while. Sagana, as though she'd seen something simply hilarious, smiled widely.

Rebecca, abandoned in the doorway, didn't like it. She didn't like it one bit. Evan was playing some sort of game with her. Was this supposed to be foreplay? He'd bought her the white shoes, declared his desire for her, and promised her a tequila evening. She couldn't just continue to stand in the doorway. She felt like a fool. She could ignore him, go straight to her room, pretend that he didn't even exist. No. There was some game afoot and she'd be a good sport, much as it irritated her. She'd show Evan that she wasn't so self-involved that she couldn't play one of his games. Yes, he could invent all the rules, decide the actions and boundaries, as long as she found it exciting. If he came to her later in bed it would all be worth it. Tequila must have some special meaning for him.

She left the doorway and approached the sofa. Sagana looked up at her. Evan didn't. Rebecca crammed her way and sat in between them. She squirmed and pushed. Nobody made room for her. She elbowed Evan in the ribs. She needed room and he was deliberately refusing to budge and she didn't have to bow to every stupid rule in his game. Sagana began to laugh. A hearty laugh. Well, that was good. It was a very full, throaty laugh, not typical of Sagana. But Evan wasn't laughing. She turned to face him. He was smiling over her head at Sagana. What an elaborate game. He stood. Balancing the bottles of tequila, he headed toward the kitchen. Rebecca heard him rummaging around; he was mixing drinks. She found herself really desiring the tequila—she could imagine its electric taste, its fire. A drink would help her get through this stupid game, which was so unlike the erotic one she'd been envisioning.

Sagana was holding her hand. How odd. Not that she and Sagana never touched. Of course they did. All the time. They'd been best friends forever. Sagana, sitting there in her black pajamas, holding her hand in the most intense way.

"I'm sorry, Becky," she said strangely.

"Sorry?"

"Yes. I am. Truly."

"For what?"

Sagana was silent.

"For what?"

Sagana smiled a radiant smile and scratched her jaw with her free hand, but said nothing. Suddenly Evan was there, standing over them, holding a tray. Sagana let go of Rebecca's hand, which was now moist. Evan's expression—was it malicious? Bowing, kissing Sagana's hand, he gave her a drink. He merely handed Rebecca hers. The glass was cold. Orange juice, tequila, and some grenadine which he must have unearthed from one of the cabinets. An exploding tequila sunrise. Neither she nor Sagana tasted their drinks. As Evan, holding his own drink carefully, wedged himself in the middle between them, Rebecca saw Sagana wipe off her hand where Evan had kissed it.

Rebecca's thigh was now positioned uncomfortably—half on the arm of the sofa and half on the seat. What an unpleasant bore this all was. Abruptly, Sagana stood, walked to the TV, placed her drink on top of it and walked in the direction of her own bedroom. Rebecca was grateful and relieved. Maybe this game between Saggie and Evan was over at last. Sagana had grown tired of pretending that she and Evan had some special understanding. Evan would simply have to come to his senses. But Sagana had already changed her mind. The drink was in her hand again and she was retracing her steps. Reclaiming her seat on the other side of Evan, she shrugged: "Why not?" She looked at her own feet. "Why not," she repeated, standing once more, hesitating, and then boldly cramming herself in the middle, joining the game of musical chairs. Some of her drink spilled. Some of Rebecca's drink also spilled. Evan managed not to spill any of his.

"A toast!" Evan cried. "I propose a toast."

"To what?" asked Rebecca irritably.

"A toast to," he smiled, "the three of us." He touched Sagana's glass with his own; she touched Rebecca's. Rebecca, sulking, reluctantly took her first sip. She took two more in quick succession. The drink was astonishingly strong. He must have tripled the usual amount of tequila. Was it a mistake? Sagana and Evan were both leaning back against the sofa pillows, sipping their drinks. They were both looking straight ahead, as though waiting for someone to arrive.

Okay. She leaned back and also looked straight ahead. She continued to work on the strong burning drink. Evan finished his drink first. An instant later

Sagana finished hers. Evan took Sagana's empty glass and stood over Rebecca, waiting for her to finish. Was this a race, a contest? She gulped the rest down, and Evan nearly snatched the glass from her hand and went back to the kitchen. Now Sagana was looking at the ceiling and Rebecca couldn't read her expression.

The room was already starting to spin. "Sagana," she said suddenly, surprising herself, "you're really pretty. I never noticed it before."

Sagana glanced at her. "My, my," she said, and then Evan was there again, a little unsteady on his feet, but with a great flourish dispensing the second round of drinks. He aimed for the middle position on the sofa and almost but not quite fell into it. Despite his awkward landing, this time the arrangement felt comfortable and easy. This tequila evening, this game . . . Why it wasn't so bad, after all.

"What do you think?" Evan asked in a tense voice.

Rebecca, surprised, saw that it was to Sagana he was speaking. And she was, she realized, as she tried to focus on the two of them, very drunk, well beyond tipsy. The room was not spinning around; it was cavorting.

"What do I think? I told you . . . why the hell not . . ." Sagana took a large swallow.

"It won't be hell. It will be heaven."

Rebecca shook her head and looked down at the rug. For a moment she was certain she saw wriggling black spiders. She blinked. No spiders.

"Beyond heaven. Transcending heaven," she could hear Evan saying.

"That's quite a promise." Was Sagana laughing, crying, snarling?

"I'll keep it. This has to happen. We've all known all along. We've wanted it all along . . ."

"Have we? All of us? For the same reasons?"

Rebecca stood. Damn them. They were speaking gibberish. It was as though the extras had suddenly jammed their way onto the screen and were hatching a plot in a foreign language against the leading lady. Damn. She grabbed the box containing her new shoes and headed toward her room. Her balance was precarious, the rug treacherous: walking, she felt like a cockeyed bird on trembling legs. And she refused to turn around to see if they were watching her. Probably not. Probably still talking nonsense. So let them. She knew what she was going to do. She was going to do exactly what she'd planned earlier. She'd start her own game.

Safe. She made it to her room. She slammed the door. Okay. Her original plan, ages ago it seemed, had been to come to Evan seductively in her brand-new white shoes. And she intended to do just that, drunk or not.

Pulling too hard, she wrenched a drawer from her bureau and then calmly watched as it fell to the floor, its contents tumbling and scattering. So what? Easier to find things that way. She plucked at things, held them up, squinted at them, then discarded them. She had to outfit herself perfectly. Not the floor-length transparent nightgown with the ruffles and the bow—she'd worn that on a night when he'd been overtired and grumpy. Not the sequined G-string; too often she played stripper for him. At first he'd really liked that game, but lately . . . Tonight she would invent something new and different for Evan.

She pulled a second drawer to the floor and rummaged through it. Finally, just the thing: a white sleeveless lace leotard . . . now you see me, now you don't. She'd bought it on a whim, months before. She'd never worn it. Still seated on the floor, she started to pull it on, then, remembering she was still dressed, had to stop, carefully remove her clothes, and then start all over again. This took all her concentration; she was perspiring.

Nude beneath the leotard, she rose and tiptoed to the mirror. Ah . . . perfect. Her nipples through the lace were like luscious roses begging to be plucked. So . . . just the leotard and the white shoes and perhaps around her throat a strand of pearls. They would call attention to her slender neck. So innocent, really . . . She'd offer the temptation of a bride. Hmm . . . better than that. She'd paint her face wildly like a whore: the brightest red on her lips, such vivid bursts of color on her cheeks that she might just have been slapped, black around her eyes, false lashes stuck on, a black beauty mark pasted on her chin right below her pouting, bee-stung lower lip . . . And gaudy, extravagant rings on every finger. Five bracelets on both wrists. And perfume . . . A perfume that smelled of . . . lilies . . . She'd drench herself with it, slap it on her breasts, inside her thighs, on her ankles and wrists. She'd be the scarlet whore and the white virgin combined.

What she needed was another drink. The time had come for her to return to the living room, to make her entrance. They were waiting for her. Sagana and Evan: her loving, adoring fans. Staggering a little, she opened the door and walked the length of the hall, placing her ringed hands against the wall to steady herself.

There they were, still sitting with the same expectant expressions on their faces, sipping from full glasses. How long had she been gone? Well, they definitely were expecting someone. It had to be her. Who else?

Humming something soft and melodic, walking dramatically, seductively, she arrived in front of them, her nude body playing hide and seek through the white lace. She placed one hand on her hip. She inhaled her own aroma—it was dizzying. She waited . . . She'd been promised a tequila evening and she'd come to get it.

Sagana was rising from the sofa. Good, oh good—thank you, as always dear Sagana, for leaving me alone with Evan, alone to make wild tequila love on the sofa, on the rug . . . With you gone, Evan will be able to ravage me on the spot. But it was to Rebecca's bedroom that Sagana was going. Rebecca's own bedroom. How could that be? Why? To clean up the mess for her? To pick up all the nightgowns and scarves from the floor?

Evan too was rising and he was following Sagana. She was alone in the living room, standing in front of the empty sofa. She felt revealed and rejected. Tears would make the black around her eyes run, but she didn't care . . . But wait, had she really been rejected? After all, Evan had gone into her bedroom. He was there, awaiting her . . . Rebecca removed the white shoes, held them in one hand and followed.

In her bed, on top of the red satin sheets, sat Evan, oblivious to the chaos of the room. He was not staring at Rebecca. She tried to focus. It was at someone else, also in the bed, that he was staring. At Sagana. Sagana sat on the red sheets, still in her black pajamas, her blonde hair messy, as though she'd been running her fingers through it. Her eyeglasses were slightly crooked. She was staring directly at Rebecca.

Evan, her lover, was on the bed with Sagana. Not with her. With Sagana. Rebecca was horrified. Hurt. Drunk. Very drunk. Excited. She leaned against the doorway. Yes, she was excited. She was watching a movie.

The man in the movie was tan and strong and he was pulling off his clothes. The woman in bed with him was also undressing. The man was tan all over. The woman, a blonde, seemed strangely still. Naked, she looked like a doll. She looked once in Rebecca's direction. Then she shut her eyes. She lay down. She held her legs tightly together. The man began to thrash and writhe over her, and she lay, immobile, like death. The man didn't seem to mind. As he pressed his body against her, he was repeating a chant, an angry sounding litany of some sort. Rebecca could make out only bits and fragments: *not her, never her, always you . . . you . . . cold . . . distant . . . now . . . you . . . want it . . .*

Rebecca was still very drunk, but not so drunk that she could keep pretending forever that Evan and Sagana entwined right in front of her were shadowy figures in a movie. Evan lay still on top of Sagana. Sagana pushed him off and sat up. She looked at Rebecca. Her voice sounded to Rebecca like both a plea and a final statement: "Rebecca, there are reasons. It's for the child. My child. I want a child. Now. You see, there are reasons."

A child? Sagana had allowed Evan inside of her in order to bear a child? But why did it have to be Evan? A child? Sagana had never let on. The thought was vulgar, repulsive. She realized she was clinging to the doorway, still in her lacy leotard. A child? She touched her own belly. If a mistake, a travesty, should ever occur somehow and she became pregnant—but it would never happen, it couldn't!—no child would survive the passage out of her body. Her body—she pressed hard on her flat stomach—simply couldn't handle it. She was built all wrong for mothering. Not her. It would never happen. But why would Sagana. . . ?

It was supposed to have been her tequila evening! She was still grasping the white shoes with one hand. She flung them away from her; they landed on top of a pile of nightgowns and feathers. Next she tore off her leotard, and then the pearls around her neck. Trampling on both, she rushed toward the bed. She needed to be touched and stroked and made love to, hard, over and over. And Evan was her man. He owed it to her.

But it was into Sagana's arms that she threw herself. Not Evan's. Sagana's arms, Sagana's body, Sagana's mouth . . . She was in Sagana's embrace, not Evan's. She was smearing her lipstick and rouge onto Sagana, not onto Evan. Sagana, whose lips tasted unfamiliar yet familiar at once. How different their kisses were now from the timid pecks of best girlfriends.

What was she doing? She had flown, as though she'd been meant to do so her whole life, into Sagana's arms, and she was kissing and kissing Sagana's blonde hair, her soft skin . . . And Sagana was accepting this, was receiving it, as though she too had been meant for nothing else but this.

Suddenly they stopped. Evan was there too. They'd forgotten about him, but he'd been on the bed the whole time. He was with them, demanding their attention, inserting his body between them. He pushed Rebecca off of Sagana. Sagana sat up. "No!" she cried angrily. "Not a second time. I'll get my child. I don't want you."

"Yes you do."

Rebecca was on the sidelines now. She could scarcely breathe.

"You do," he repeated, sounding almost delirious with passion.

164

Rebecca lay on her back and looked up at the ceiling. She heard a slap. And suddenly Evan was on top of her, one side of his face distorted and scarlet. Only a moment before, in Sagana's arms, she'd been wet and flowing, but now she was drying up, closing, folding in on herself. He was inside of her. It hurt. Yet she didn't stop him. Why didn't she stop him? Why didn't Sagana? In seconds it was over. He rolled off her. Her thighs were sticky. She felt poisoned.

Sagana, still naked and glistening, was stroking her forehead. "Becky," she said softly, "it's all right. But now you have to choose."

Evan laughed, his hand on his inflamed cheek.

Sagana wanted her to choose. Evan was still laughing. Rebecca turned to stare at Sagana. "You," she whispered.

"Get out now." Sagana was in total, supreme command, haughty, regal . . . "Get out!"

Evan had been banished, but he managed to smirk even as he obeyed the command of one who was to become a Queen, an Amazon. He bowed. "For my lady love, I'll go. But we'll be together soon."

"If so, on my terms."

And she and Sagana were alone. Sagana stroked her forehead, then her neck, her throat, her breasts . . . And Rebecca felt herself coming alive again, felt her body growing slippery with desire. Where would the desire lead her? To a place she'd always wanted, always . . . She moaned, the first real moan of her life, the first one ever because she couldn't stop herself, not simply to excite a partner . . . She wrapped her legs around Sagana and then they were twisting and clinging, dancers, lovers, twins.

Sagana was whispering to her, kissing her, then speaking, then kissing her again, the same fiery passion in both her kisses and her words. But her kisses were understandable; the words were riddles.

"You're an innocent . . . and a demon . . . My love . . . my rage . . ."

The words were patter. They didn't count. What counted now was that Sagana was tenderly biting her breasts. She would bite her and speak, bite her and speak, in a patterned movement, like a dance. Sagana had called her an innocent—she had heard those words, had understood that much—and now Sagana's teeth were urgently at her breasts.

Sagana's tongue was lapping gently, probing, discovering . . . But she wanted her turn now at giving. She rose. Without looking at Sagana's face, she gently pushed her down on the bed. She was going to do the same for Sagana. She'd been born to do this. Sagana would taste velvety, soft, like raspberry sherbet . . . Sagana would taste exactly as she, herself, would taste. She looked at Sagana, who looked back at her. Sagana—a woman in bed with her—but really there was nothing so frightening about being with a woman. It was simply like being with herself, if she inhabited two bodies at once. There was something so tantalizing about the idea. A perfect total lovemaking, all encompassing. Beneath their different exteriors, she and Sagana were twins with the potential to become one. Two women, two beautiful women, two mirrors: the same woman.

Now she wanted to kiss and lick and smother with her mouth the bird, that enchanting birthmark on Sagana's hip. Always, before, when she'd caught a glimpse of it, she'd thought it just an oddity—a slightly askew, misplaced bird. But now she saw how beautiful it was. First she kissed the flesh of Sagana's hip, and

166

even though it was harder and firmer than her own, it was so very much like her own. The feeling made her dizzy. Her tongue darted out and she licked the bird so slightly, just grazed it with her tongue, and Sagana was moaning and crying, her fists grasping the sheet, and Rebecca looked up and saw Sagana's face distorted with passion, aflame, and she felt herself quickly moving to the same point. She covered Sagana with her body, thrust her body against Sagana's, and placed her lips to Sagana's neck.

They lay side by side. Moments passed. Rebecca dared to open her eyes. Sagana, on one elbow, was watching her intently. Catlike, Rebecca stretched.

"Am I beautiful, Saggie?" she asked, surprised that Sagana wasn't already crooning endearments to her, as men did after lovemaking.

Tenderly, Sagana began to stroke her hair. "Of course you are, Becky. You know that."

Rebecca fanned out her hair. She wanted Sagana to continue to stroke her, to caress her. She expected to be petted and coddled.

"Which part of me do you find the most beautiful?"

Sagana's fingers paused, then continued their gentle stroking motion. "All of you. You know that."

"But do you like my eyes most? My hair? Or is it . . . my breasts . . ." She felt her own nipples harden, and raising her head stared at her breasts. So full, so lovely. She glanced at Sagana's breasts—not quite as full, not quite as appealing. Sagana was not, then, exactly a mirror, not exactly a reflection.

Sagana said nothing. Slowly, much more slowly now, she continued to stroke Rebecca's hair.

"Saggie, what did it feel like for you, though? Was I . . . really . . . exciting?"

167

Abruptly, Sagana's fingers stopped. "Becky . . ." She shook her head, but didn't finish the sentence.

Rebecca was annoyed. Sagana was not saying the right things. She seemed so reluctant to flatter and pamper her. Men always knew what to say afterwards. She pouted. "Where's Evan?"

Pulling back, Sagana looked at her.

"Where is he? He must still be here." She was sure now that Evan would want her again. The delirium which had taken hold of him would have passed, and now he would choose her again, choose her over . . . anyone else. Sagana had wanted her, and Evan would too, now, at this moment, just as he had in the past. She and Evan could still rescue their very own tequila evening. Sagana had told her to choose, but that didn't mean that she was bound to that choice eternally.

"Do you know where Evan is?"

In answer, Sagana rose from the bed. Was she going to find Evan for her, to bring him to her? No, she guessed not, because Sagana stood still and tall, her legs wide apart, her body slick with perspiration, her eyes flashing with anger.

Rebecca was afraid to move, to blink, to breathe, to do anything. What had happened? She'd made a terrible mistake!

Sagana turned on her heel and was gone from the room. Still afraid to move, Rebecca stayed as she was. Maybe Sagana would return. Finally she could stand it no more. Not bothering to dress, she ran into the living room, where the three empty tequila glasses sat. The room looked unfamiliar, threatening. She wasn't the least bit drunk anymore. She ran to Sagana's room and threw open the door. The apartment was empty. Evan had gone and Sagana too had vanished. She was abandoned. Slumping against the wall, she knew that she would come down with a fever. She wanted to. She wanted a fever that would last for weeks and that would erase the memory of this night. And the memory of how she had lost Sagana.

She jumped. Through the glass, she heard the bird squawk loudly. She shivered. The sound was so unexpected and jarring that she came to herself, came back to the present. So she had remembered at last after all this time. No fever could erase that memory permanently. A burden had been lifted. She'd lifted it herself. And she felt almost calm.

The bird squawked again, less belligerently, and began to preen, using its sharp silvery beak to smooth its feathers.

This was not the worst time to remember. No, in fact it was the very best time. Not that she had any choice in the matter. Not at all. It had chosen to come to her. She had lived through it one more time, but this time she had emerged . . . strong. With a flurry, the bird spread its wings and flew to a higher perch. Rebecca stared up at the dark evening sky, then back at the bird, and then forced herself to walk.

Sagana had returned after that night only to give birth and to wait for the time to leave for the mountain as the Amazon Queen. She and Sagana had never spoken of that night during the months that followed. Not once—even though both Lily and Diana had been conceived that night.

Rebecca paused, then walked, then stopped again. On the sidewalk directly in front of her sprawled a disheveled man, and she had to concentrate and step around him. She was reminded that she was alone, walking along dark city streets. She had chosen evening for the meeting time to show Sagana that danger no longer frightened her, but now she felt connected to the life of the city once more. She no longer felt detached, invulnerable.

In the street a police car raced past, its siren wailing. She shuddered, but kept walking. She turned left. The light was red. She waited. Glancing in the window of a cafe, she saw people—lovers, friends—sipping drinks and laughing. Was it possible that she and Sagana would soon, one day, go out together for a drink? Perhaps later tonight, she and Saggie and Howard would be sitting around a table, eating and drinking. They would be laughing and chatting. About what, though? What in the world was she actually going to say to Sagana? How could any words possibly convey what she felt, when she herself wasn't even sure of her feelings? "I'm sorry, Saggie," she could begin, "Let's be friends . . . No, I'm not sorry at all . . . We *are* friends, you know, despite it all . . . And by the way, who are we?"

The light changed. She crossed the street. None of those were right. There would be no readymade script to rehearse and memorize en route, no stock phrases. She began to tremble slightly; how very close to her destination she was!

Ahead, outside a club, waiting for the evening's show, stood a long line of teenagers in garish clothes: black leather jackets decorated with studs and patches and glittering silver boots. Perhaps Howard had stood right here, outside this very club, not so long ago, before he'd run off to the mountain.

Now she was across the street from the park itself.

She didn't want to look at it, though. She felt too panicked. Clenching her fists, she looked up at the sky instead. It was night blue, midnight blue, with the street lamps taking the place of stars. Deliberately unclenching her fists, she began to walk again, but slowly now, extremely slowly. She looked at the runners on the periphery of the park, not into the park itself. Runners seemed to be everywhere—she was surrounded by them, in their slinky nylon shorts, multi-colored sneakers, with headphones over their ears . . .

At the entrance, she stopped, her heart racing, and finally looked inside. The park was filled with people. She could just make out the broad, sturdy arch, but not its details, not the carved eagle on top nor the coats of arms on either side. Beneath the arch she imagined a steel band playing, their music echoing eerily, or a mime in whiteface wearing a bowler hat gracefully pantomiming the everyday actions of the individuals crowded around . . . And the crowd would be applauding and laughing. Somewhere, lost in the crowd or standing on the sidelines, Sagana and Howard awaited her. She took a deep breath, paused for a few runners to pass, and entered Washington Square.

Her pace quickened slightly and she was breathing deeply, deliberately. Together, she and Sagana and Howard would begin to discover how much they each loved one another. They would discover which fears connected them, which hopes they shared. Together, they would begin to remove the layers of disguise they'd each worn.

The arch was closer now, and she was beginning to hear the music; not a steel band, but something not easily identifiable, a haunting sound, high-pitched and tremulous, erratic and pulsing. With the sounds of this strange music, she began moving more rapidly, more and more quickly, until she was nearly running. Although she was still a mystery, she was not forever unfathomable, and she was growing closer, with every step, not only to Sagana and Howard, but to herself.